BODY IN THE CANAL

Detectives tackle a murky case of murder

DIANE M. DICKSON

THE
BOOK
FOLKS

Published by The Book Folks

London, 2022

ISBN 978-1-80462-042-7

www.thebookfolks.com

BODY IN THE CANAL is the fifth standalone title in the DI Jordan Carr mystery series.

A list of characters can be found at the back of this book.

For Paul F - Thank you.

Prologue

It had been a miserable, wet day. The rain was thin and feeble but still heavy enough to soak everything through and cause the gutters to overflow, and windows to be streaked and smeared. Early summer blossoms were ruined; bright petals bruised and delicate buds discoloured. It had been a fine spring but today was a better reflection of the current circumstances. Fear and grief still stalked the streets and the future felt like a threat.

In the city, the lights from the shops fell softly onto slick pavements. Out of town, on the canal bank, the soil was sodden and dark. Trees dripped, and the surface of the canal dimpled.

Jean Barker felt stale and stuffy after being indoors all day so, in spite of the rain, she went for a walk along the bank passing under the old bridges.

It was a quiet afternoon. Everyone was inside, keeping dry, staying safe. It was hard to tell one day from the other nowadays. Things were improving slowly but there were still many people staying at home, working in their bedrooms and kitchens. Yet Jean had been desperate for a breath of cool damp air.

When Ben had been alive, they used to walk in the rain often, striding out, blood pulsing, and then they'd call in for a drink at the pub. She wouldn't do that right now. They had opened up now that the pandemic lockdowns were over and an attempt was made at normality but for her it wasn't the same. Ben was gone as was Jess, the dog. Now, really quite suddenly, as she remembered, Jean felt lonely. She paused for a minute and looked around. She could hear children playing in a garden somewhere, and now and then, on the other side, behind the overgrown hedge, and the metal fence, there was the glint of metal as a car drove down the road, or a bike swished through the wet.

She'd go home, ring Mel. It was always possible that she'd be working. It was hard to keep a track of her shifts especially now with the hospitals still so busy and the staff exhausted by extra hours and extended shifts.

Never mind, there was always the chance that they could have a chat and finalise plans for her visit. Jean couldn't wait. It had been far too long, weeks turning into months of worry about her daughter, who worked as a nurse. At the sharp end.

She climbed the steps to the road. Up ahead a narrowboat had moored alongside the bank. It was impossible to tell whether or not there was anyone aboard. All the little windows were covered with curtains. It looked picturesque beside the water, and she took out her phone to get a picture. As she lined up the shot headlights swept around the bend. Too fast. People always drove too fast. She forgot about the barge and stepped back towards the wall, waiting a moment for safety. There was just a quick thrill of unease as the vehicle flew past spraying grey water across the pavement and soaking her trousers and shoes.

"You stupid bugger!" she yelled after the disappearing taillights.

It slowed just for a moment and then sped away. She turned for home and when the same vehicle swept past again, she raised two fingers as it disappeared again at the end of the road. She laughed to herself. Ben would have been appalled at the gesture, but the driver had really annoyed her. He was gone now but she felt better for expressing her anger.

Chapter 1

Melanie Barker couldn't decide between irritation or worry. They'd arranged this visit home a month ago and Mam said she'd collect her. Yet here she was at Liverpool's Lime Street station, standing next to Ken Dodd, frozen in time, and no sign of her mother. She'd phoned repeatedly on the way and the phone was either switched off or the battery flat. It didn't matter particularly. She could just get the train to Old Roan station, but they'd agreed. She was tired and looking forward to a drink. The train from Manchester had been okay, not crowded, with space to keep away from other passengers, which wasn't as essential as it had been a few months ago but still preferable. A local train to Old Roan would only take twenty minutes but it would be more crowded, and she'd have to walk down to Central and she really didn't fancy it. It seemed that now there was no choice.

When she arrived at the house, she didn't bother to ring the bell. She gave one knock on the door out of politeness, and then used her own key. She dropped her overnight bag on the floor and called out. There was no response.

"Mam, it's me. Are you alright?"

The living room was empty. She ran upstairs expecting to find her mother in bed. The spectre of the virus raised its head. There must be something wrong because Jean was a tough woman who 'got on with things'. She didn't let much get her down.

There was no-one in the bedroom. The bathroom door was open showing another empty space. She glanced into the box room, her own bedroom. Nothing.

There was nobody in the kitchen. The back door was unlocked, the key still in the latch. Mel ran into the garden. Again, nothing to see.

Back in the living room the fire was unlit. There was a book open on the settee and a cup and plate on the coffee table. It was unlike Mam to leave those out but maybe things had slid a bit during the months of lockdown and loneliness. Having company would soon get things back to normal.

Had she been taken ill? Had she gone to the doctor? The walk-in centre? Surely if an ambulance had been called, they would have let her know. Where the hell was she? She dialled the mobile number. The phone rang out but there was no echo in any of the rooms. She left another voicemail message, this one with deepening panic.

This was very wrong. Mam's dressing gown was on the hook at the back of her bedroom door. Her handbag was on the chair in the corner. Her glasses were nowhere.

So, what the hell was she supposed to do now? Go to the neighbours' just in case Mam had gone to Mrs Clough's next door? Unlikely, but all of this was unlikely.

She would ring the Royal. She would be kept on hold, maybe for hours. If they were as busy as her own hospital in Manchester, they wouldn't thank her for taking up time on the off chance that Jean was a patient. Surely, if they had admitted her mother, they would have let her know. That left the police. She should ring the police. Mam would be livid if the police were round and all she'd done was nip to the shop.

She would ring Penny. Her mate would advise her. Penny's hubby was a policeman, something special from what she'd been told. Not just a bobby. She'd never met him, but she'd been in university with Penny and now and then they still connected on Facebook and Twitter. Yes. Penny herself worked with Citizens Advice. She'd tell her what to do.

Chapter 2

"I'm sorry to bother you, Pens. Are you in work?"

"No it's fine. I'm on my way home. Just picked up Harry from the nursery. Hey, it's great to hear from you. What's going on?"

"I need a bit of advice. I'm at my mam's."

"Oh right. How is she?"

"Well, that's it. I don't know. I haven't been down for months. We've been so busy and then in the early days I didn't want to risk bringing the virus to her. But I thought it was probably okay now we've both been jabbed and boosted. She's been on her own all the time and she was really looking forward to a couple of days with company. But she's not here. Listen, let me start from the beginning."

As she went through the story Mel struggled to keep the panic from her voice.

"I don't know where she is. I'm trying to keep calm, you know. I'm trying to be sensible but it's just so odd."

"Ring the police. That's what you should do. Find the number of the local station and tell them all about it."

"Do you really think I should? I mean, she's not a kid."

"Of course you should. Maybe it's not a problem. In fact I'm sure it's not and you're going to be having a laugh about this soon. But with what you told me I reckon you need at least some proper help from them. Will you be able to find the number of the local station?"

"I dunno. Oh yes, of course I can. Jesus, look at me. I'm supposed to be a calm professional and I'm acting like a hysterical teenager."

"Look, I've just arrived home and Jordan's car is here so he must be in before me. That's a miracle in itself. I'll ask him who you should ring. Hang up for now and I'll call you back in a couple of minutes. Don't worry. I'm sure it's all fine."

* * *

Jordan was in the kitchen making some soup.

"You're home early," Penny said.

"I was in court all afternoon and I have to be at the station first thing in the morning, so I skived off for an hour. Dave Griffiths was doing the same. I thought, well, sauce for the goose and all that."

He walked through to meet them and picked up Harry who was giggling and squirming.

"Are you okay, love?" Jordan said. "You look a bit flustered."

"I need your help."

"Okay."

"Do you remember Mel, I was at uni with her? Anyway, we were close at one time and we speak now on Facebook and on the phone now and again. She's just rung me in a bit of a state. Apparently, she's come down to see her mum, Jean, and she's not there. It's all a bit strange."

Jordan listened until he'd heard the full story. "Well, love, you gave her the best advice you could. I'm sure her mum will turn up and it'll all be explained. These things usually are."

"I know, but she sounded really worried. She's nice, you haven't met her I don't think, but she was really kind to me at uni. I had a bit of a wobble before my finals, and she was just brilliant. We don't keep in close contact but she's a mate, you know."

"Tell you what, love. Why don't you go and see to Harry, and I'll give her a ring and have a chat with her. Do you think that might help?"

"Please." She stood on her toes and gave him a quick kiss. "Then we can have that soup and watch a film. I'm sorry to spoil what should have been a couple of hours off."

"Don't be daft. It's no problem. Go on, put the lad to bed, he's falling asleep on the floor in the living room."

Chapter 3

"Hello, is that Mel?"

Jordan stood in the kitchen stirring the soup. He'd used Penny's phone so that the number would be recognised. For convenience he'd scribbled a couple of numbers on the noticeboard above the table.

"Yes, hello. I guess that's Jordan. I'm really sorry to bother you. I'm probably being a silly mare and panicking about nothing."

"Well, you obviously have some concerns and I'm not surprised from what Penny just told me. I'm not saying there is anything to be unduly worried about, we just need to make sure your mum's okay. Have you tried the neighbours?"

"Not yet. On one side they are new and she doesn't know them very well. Mrs Clough has been here forever but she's a real old biddy. Mam talks to her sometimes, but they're not friends."

"I think it might be worthwhile you just popping round there. Even if your mum isn't there, they might have seen her."

"Oh, right – I should do that then, should I?"

Jordan glanced at his watch. It was still early. He heard his son giggling as he and Penny ran from the bathroom into the little bedroom. He turned the heat off under the pan.

"I'll tell you what. Why don't I come round there and see what's what? Only if you want me to, of course. Otherwise I can give you the number for Copy Lane Police Station and they'll maybe send a patrol. I could ring them myself, of course, but I'd rather get a clear idea of the situation before I do that."

"I'd be really, really grateful. I'm trying to hold it together, but I just feel like there's something wrong."

"Text me your mum's address and I'll be with you in a little while. Try not to worry."

He shouted up the stairs and Penny appeared on the landing.

"Do you think there's something wrong?" she said.

Jordan shrugged. "Difficult to say but your friend is upset so I'll go and see what I can do."

"You're a star, you really are."

"Yeah well. If I'm not back in a couple of hours have your dinner and keep the soup warm for me."

He blew her a kiss.

* * *

The traffic was thinning after the evening rush. It was less than twenty minutes before Jordan turned onto the Dunnings Bridge Road, and then into the Old Roan housing estate.

The semi-detached houses had obviously been owned by the council before Mrs Thatcher interfered. It wasn't a bad area though. He had driven past fields to get here and there were some old established trees lining the pavements, and most of the gardens were well kept.

Jean Barker's house was neat. Her small white car was pulled onto the tarmac drive which answered one of his questions but in a way that made the situation possibly more sinister.

The door opened as he parked beside the kerb and Melanie Barker stepped out onto the path. She was tense and Jordan saw, as he came closer, that her eyes were red and puffy. She was struggling to hold back even more tears.

Chapter 4

Mel could barely wait until they were inside before she started her breathless account.

"I've checked, she isn't at the neighbours'. Mrs Clough – Lily – saw her on Tuesday. Mam picked up some stuff from the Asda for her. Lily said the car's not moved since. She hardly goes out at the moment – something to do with her knees – and she spends loads of time just looking out the window."

"Okay. What sort of things does your mum like to do? Does she go jogging or anything, cycling?"

"No, nothing like that. She goes to a yoga group. It had to stop for a while, but I think they are starting it back. Not sure when, mind you. Like I said on the phone to Pen, she was lonely while we were locked down."

"Okay," Jordan said. He waited a moment and looked at Mel directly. "Don't read anything into this, it's just a question. Has your mum been depressed enough to perhaps want to go away on her own?" He was avoiding what he needed to ask. He took a breath, then asked, "Has she ever given you the idea that she might not want to carry on?"

"Carry on?" Mel said. "How do you mean? Oh God. No, no. Shit, I never even thought. No. Not Mam. She'd never do anything like that. She'd never kill herself."

Jordan held out a hand. "As I said, Mel, it was just a question, something I had to ask. If we do bring in Copy Lane, they will ask you similar questions. We always do. You can see why. Not because we especially think she may have done something to herself, but we need to have an idea of her state of mind. I'm sorry, love."

The tears that Mel had been fighting won the battle now and she brushed them aside with the back of her hand.

"No. I'm okay, I really am. I understand but she just wouldn't. Yes, she was a bit lonely but she's resilient, kept herself busy. In fairness she's been like that since my dad died. They were very close. But anyway, she reads loads and she does the garden and… well, it's been tough for everyone, but she was coping."

"Good. You seem pretty sure about that, so have a think. Is there anything she's mentioned lately that was out of the ordinary. Did anything happen that upset her or worried her?"

"Not that I can think of. We talked a few times a week. There wasn't much to say really. I was working and when I wasn't working, I was so bloody whacked I was sleeping, and Mam, well she was just plodding on."

There was a rattle from the kitchen at the end of the hallway.

"Oh that must be Percy. I wondered where he'd gone."

"Percy?"

"The cat. I hadn't seen him and he's usually around. Out in the garden or in the kitchen." They heard the scratch of a dish on the tiles and Mel dredged up a smile. "He'll want something to eat. That's another thing. His dish is empty and not washed out, you know, it had stuff stuck on it. She never leaves it like that, and his water bowl was dry."

"Let's go through there and you can sort him out. We can talk about what's happened and what I reckon you should do next."

Mel spooned out cat food from a foil container as the cat wound between her ankles.

"This is probably going to sound a bit odd but just bear with me, Mel," Jordan said.

"Okay."

"Has your mum ever done anything like this before?"

"How do you mean, like this?"

"Has she ever gone off on her own without letting you know?"

"No, no, of course not. She's not like that. She keeps in touch. We're close. Even more since Da died. I mean, yes, I'm in Manchester, but she used to come and see me, and I come home when I can. That's just daft, that idea."

"Okay. Have you checked her wardrobe to see if she's taken anything with her?"

"No, I haven't. Why would I do that? I've just said, she would have let me know."

"Mel, if we decide that we should make this official, report it to the local station, these are all questions that you'll be asked. So, if we've covered them first it'll make things move more smoothly."

"I'll go and check. Oh there was one thing. There's a pot by the back door. Daffodils. It's been kicked over. It's just lying there with the soil and broken flowers. Mam is fussy about the garden. She wouldn't have just left that."

"Was the back door unlocked?"

"Yes, it was. She is a bit careless about it. I'm always on at her. Oh God, where is she? What's happened?"

Chapter 5

Jordan listened to the sound of Mel in the bedroom and bathroom upstairs. He was unsettled after speaking to her. It could be that something was wrong here. He sent a message to Penny letting her know he wouldn't be back for a while.

As Mel thundered down the stairs, he was in the hall waiting. She held up a brown leather bag.

"This is Mam's. She wouldn't have gone far without it. She never does. I've teased her that it's grafted to her shoulder."

"Right, we need to go through it," Jordan said.

Mel looked down at the bag. "It's funny, that feels really wrong. Ever since I was little, I was told not to go in it. I suppose she had things that could have hurt me. Scissors maybe, or aspirins. Anyway it's sort of stuck with me. It feels all wrong. Oh well here we go."

She tipped the contents onto the kitchen table and began to sort through them – packets of tissues, a manicure set, old tickets.

"There's nothing here that looks unusual." As she spoke, she pushed her hand into a small pocket. "Oh. Bloody hell." She dragged out a mobile phone. "It's flat."

"Is that her current phone, the one that she's using at the moment?"

"I'm not sure. I suppose it must be. I mean, I don't know why she'd have more than one."

They found the charger in a drawer in the kitchen. "Give it a couple of minutes to charge."

"All my calls are on here. So that's pretty clear, this is her current phone. Why would she go out without it? I mean, she's not glued to it like most of us, but she usually has it with her." She shook her head.

"Is there anything else?"

Jordan waited as Mel scrolled through the menus.

"I don't really know what I'm looking for. There's some stuff about the yoga class starting back up. Doctor's appointment, the dentist. Nothing dead important. Perhaps you should have a look."

As she spoke Mel held the phone out for Jordan to take.

"Come on, let's get things started." He walked through to the kitchen and filled a tumbler with cold water. "Here, have this." He pulled a chair from under the table, took out his notebook and flipped it open.

"Best thing is to alert the local nick and then I reckon I'll go down and have a word with them. Will you be okay here on your own? It would be best if there's someone here just in case your mum comes back."

"Oh please, God, let's hope she does."

Jordan stepped into the hallway to make the call.

"That's good news," he said as he came back into the kitchen. "I've just spoken to them and I was able to speak to DS Stella May. She's someone I've worked with before. She's brilliant. I'm going down to have a word with her. We'll get things moving."

"How do you mean?"

"My thoughts right now are that it is possible your mum is out there and unable to let you know. The local nick will have contacts with hospitals and what have you, and if necessary, they are best placed to take it further. But let me go and have a word with Stella. She's waiting for me. I'll be back as soon as I can, but you've got my number and if you're worried at all, ring me immediately. Okay?"

"Yeah. I'll go and tidy up a bit in the living room."

"Actually, it would probably be better if you just leave things as they are for the time being."

Jordan watched the look of fear as Mel caught up with his thinking as she became more aware of the truth of the situation. There was nothing he could do to reassure her.

Chapter 6

Detective Sergeant Stella May was waiting in the doorway near the car park. Jordan waved as he crossed the tarmac. There was a moment of awkwardness as she held out a hand and Jordan opened both arms. They laughed and she stepped forward to wrap her arms around him; she even gave him a quick peck on the cheek.

"Probably completely out of order that," Jordan said. "Not only are we still supposed to be keeping distanced wherever possible but there's all the physical contact stuff as well. But we had some hairy moments together back in Kirkby. I think we should be excused." Jordan glanced around as he stepped back. "No cameras here, are there?"

"Oh yes, loads. We're probably going on report right now." Stella laughed. "Nobody hugs anymore. It's good to see you, Jordan."

"And you. I was really pleased when I found out you were here. How long is it since your transfer?"

"Couple of months now. They reckon there's more chance of me getting a promotion – when I've put my time in. One of the DIs is retiring next year so with luck I might slot in. Anyway, it was gone time for a change. I'd been in Kirkby since I was in uniform, plus this is nearer my gaff."

"Oh that's right. Are you still in your flat, up by the racecourse?"

"Yep. Still there."

"And is the physio guy still upstairs? I liked him."

"Yeah, he is. We're having the place upgraded. Loads of work going on. It's a tip right now but it'll be ace when it's finished."

"Oh, nice. Your landlord paying for it, I hope."

"Well no. I bought it. So…"

"Wow. Congratulations."

Stella smiled and stepped backwards into the corridor.

"So, your missing lady. No sign of her yet?"

"No. The daughter's out of her mind with worry. I have to say that it's looking a bit dodgy the more I learn."

"Well, it's very early."

"It is but the last time she was seen was Tuesday."

"Hmmm, under the circumstances I'll get a statement from the daughter and prepare a report, well" – she shrugged – "you know the drill."

"Thanks. I suppose I could have told her to wait but it does ring a few alarm bells. So, what else are you working on just now?"

"A weird one, pretty nasty. We've got a young woman fished out of the cut. Come on down to the incident room and I'll show you a copy of the PM report. It's pretty grotty I have to say. Poor thing hadn't been having a very good time."

The room was almost empty. A couple of whiteboards had been set up with images of the victim. Some had been taken at the crime scene, the body laid on wet grass. In the other pictures she was mostly covered by a white sheet. Her face was pale, her eyes closed, and there was the tip of a scar showing on the right shoulder, the end of the Y incision. She had been pretty, and Jordan was relieved that he hadn't been present for this post-mortem examination.

"Where is she from?" Jordan asked.

"We haven't got much at all to go on. There was no ID on the body. She was in the Leeds-Liverpool just up the road. She'd been in the canal a short while. A dog walker found her and dragged her out, even tried CPR but it was way too late."

"Ah that explains the way the body was laid out. I wondered about that."

"Yes, she meant well, and it was perfectly innocent. We've interviewed her and there's nothing suspicious there. Anyway, right now we're doing fingertip searches on the bank and ground nearby. Divers are going in tomorrow. We've had to wait until they had a team free. I'm starting house-to-house enquiries and there's going to be a piece in the *Echo*. As always, the first thing is to find out who the victim was, and we'll move on from there."

Stella shifted across to look at the picture of the woman. Her hair was scraped back from her face and flowed over the edge of the steel table. There were a couple of red marks on her cheek and on a close-up shot of the woman's neck a red line stood out stark against the pale skin.

"See this?" Stella said as she pointed out the red mark.

"Strangled?" he asked. "Or maybe hanged."

"You'd think, wouldn't you? But no. This was not the cause of death. I'll get to that. The medical examiner reckons this is the mark of a collar, some hard material because it's rubbed the skin clean off in some places."

"A collar? What, you mean her clothes did that?"

"No. More like a collar that a dog would wear. From what we've seen it looks as if she was chained up. There's bruising on one ankle. The thinking right now is that she was restrained with a collar round her neck and possibly some sort of shackle. Her knees and the tops of her feet are rubbed raw." Here Stella pointed to another image. "It looks as if this poor sod was kept like some sort of animal. Crawling around on a hard floor."

Jordan blew out his cheeks and shook his head. "Bloody Nora. That's horrible."

"It is."

"What was the cause of death?"

"Blunt trauma. Could have been the result of a fall. She was found just by one of the bridges, could have jumped and cracked her head on the parapet. That is more likely than an actual deliberate blow. There were bits of stone in the wound, we're having it matched with stuff from the bridge."

"So suicide?"

Stella shrugged. "It's so strange that I'm having trouble settling on a scenario. She could have jumped in deliberately, of course. But if she'd been kept captive and escaped, why do that? Why not just get help? She could have been pushed, I suppose, or she could have been running scared. There are too many options right now. Anyway, come on and have a cup of coffee. And you can tell me all about your mate's mother."

"Not really my friend. She was at uni with Penny, and I don't know much to be honest. This woman" – he jerked a thumb back toward the images – "would you mind letting me have a look at what you have? It's intriguing."

"Of course, help yourself. I would welcome any ideas that you might have. We're right at the start. Only had her for about twelve hours."

Chapter 7

Stella sipped at her coffee in silence as Jordan read through the report. He laid it to one side and rubbed his hands over his face.

"Undernourished, dehydrated, marks from long-standing restraint. Thickened skin on her knees probably the result of repeated rubbing, likely the result of crawling on a hard floor. Jesus, what happened to this woman?"

Stella gathered the papers together and slid them into a folder.

"I guess that's one of the many things I have to find out. Interesting there was no violence – unless of course you consider tying someone up like a dog violent – which I do, but no beating or anything like that."

"And you have no idea where she came from?" Jordan asked.

Stella shook her head. "I've sent the guys home because we've spent ages going through CCTV. They were all boss-eyed. A lot of that area is residential, and we don't even know which direction she came from. We've got the team grabbing copies of any security cameras from the shops and the station, but I don't know how far my spread should be. It's the Melling Road bridge so I don't think she came from the motorway.

"Anyway I'm increasing the house-to-house tomorrow when more people will be home. It's a decent area, always has been. There's the usual number of car thefts, a few break-ins, but it's not like– well, you know what some estates are like. We don't even know how she arrived. If she was on foot, we're going to be bloody lucky to spot her. She was barefoot and she wore just a skirt and jumper, scruffy but not enough to attract too much attention. Some of the wounds on her feet were recent so she could have walked or run. Added to that, she was in the water and that'll have washed away some evidence. Dirt, pollen, anything like that. The medical examiner did get stuff from under the fingernails and toenails."

"Have you got a decent-sized team?"

"There're never enough bods, are there? But I've got some civilians and a few new bods. I miss Rupert Moon. He's got his promotion by the way. He's still in Kirkby. The DCI here, Josh Martin, is very supportive. Do you know him?"

Jordan shook his head.

"This is terrible," he said. "If I can be any help just let me know."

"Thanks, but we should be concentrating on Jean Barker right now. I need to speak to the daughter. I'll come over with you if that's okay."

"Great idea. Have you got your car? You can follow me."

"Yep."

Out in the car park Jordan looked around for Stella's old banger and was surprised when she plipped her key and a VW ID.5 hybrid sprung to life, the lights blinking at them from the corner.

"New car?"

"Yeah. The old one was on its last legs, and I reckoned I should get something planet-friendly."

"Do you like it?"

"It's ace. Got all sorts of bells and whistles. A bit of luxury, you know."

"Is it leased?"

"No, I bought it. Look, Jordan, there's something I need to tell you. There was something that happened round about the time we were working together. I don't spread it around, but I had a bit of luck. I'll explain it when we have a minute."

"That sounds intriguing."

"No, it's not really, but let's get off and see Jean Barker's daughter, shall we?"

Chapter 8

As they pulled into the kerb in the Old Roan area the front door flew open.

Mel Barker stormed along the path towards them. "Did you find anything?"

"No but I've brought DS May back with me," Jordan said. "Let's go inside and talk about it. Obviously, you haven't heard from your mum."

"No, can't you do more than this? Can't you go on the telly? I could do one of those appeals. We have to do something."

"We need to take it step by step, Mel. There's no point going at it like a bull in a china shop."

"No. No that's not good enough. Sorry, sorry, Jordan, I know you're doing me a favour being here and I really do appreciate it, but I don't know where she is. I don't know if she's scared, maybe she's hurt. We have to find her."

"I understand, I really do," he said. "We will do everything we can, but we have routines to follow, things we've learned from experience. Look at it this way, if we were to go off now where would we even look?"

She had no answer for him. She wrapped her arms around herself pulling her cardigan tight. She turned back towards the house and trudged to the front door. Jordan glanced at Stella and raised his eyebrows.

"Poor sod. I'd be just as frantic, I reckon," Stella murmured.

After he'd introduced Stella, Jordan went into the kitchen to put the kettle on and make yet another cup of coffee. He thought maybe being on her own with the DS would be calmer and easier. While he was alone, he examined the back door. There wasn't any sign of damage to the lock or frame. He pulled it open. Beside the step there was a broken plant pot. The plant and soil were scattered on the side path. Maybe it was meaningful, maybe it was simply that the cat had knocked it over. He stepped outside and bent down closer to the scattered earth.

With his phone camera he took a couple of pictures and then went back into the kitchen where he'd seen a few plastic boxes upturned to drain beside the sink. He carried the biggest one outside and placed it gently over the pile of soil and then picked up a small rock which was sitting in the flower bed. He put that on top of the box.

When he carried the tray of drinks into the living room Mel was calmer and Stella was writing in her notebook.

He waited until Mel finished talking.

"I think you should get your team round here, Stella. Maybe get a SOC technician in and have them take a look at the soil by the back door." He handed over his phone with the image already on the screen. "That looks like a footprint to me. What size shoes does your mum take, Mel? Do you know?"

"She's a five like me. We sometimes borrow each other's shoes. Why?"

"I reckon that's bigger than a size five and it looks wider than a woman's shoe. What do you think, Stella?"

Stella nodded. "Yeah. Sorry, Mel. Don't let's jump to conclusions but I reckon we have to consider the possibility that your mum didn't go off of her own accord."

Mel didn't answer but her eyes filled with tears.

"Let me get you a nip of that brandy I saw in the kitchen, shall I? It'll make you feel better," Jordan said.

Mel nodded and as he walked down the hallway, he heard Stella telling the young woman that she was going to move things along quickly and that she was initiating an investigation immediately.

Chapter 9

It was well past midnight before Jordan made it home. He expected Penny to be in bed, but she was sitting in the living room with a glass of rum and a hot chocolate.

"Are you hungry, love?"

"No. I don't think so. I'm past eating, it's too late. I wouldn't mind one of those though." Jordan pointed at the mug.

"Have this one, it's still hot. I'll make another for me. Do you want a brandy, rum, anything?"

"I'll put a splash in here." As he spoke Jordan opened a bottle and poured a glug of brandy into his drink.

"I'll just be a minute and then you can tell me what's happening. Is Mel's mum home? Is she okay?"

Jordan just shook his head. "Afraid not. It's looking very worrying."

"Oh bugger."

While he waited for Penny, Jordan scrolled through the messages on his phone. There were a couple from DCI David Griffiths finalising arrangements for the next day which was just a few short hours away. Meetings with the lawyers and the team before one of the major cases went to court. There was one from Stella May.

> *I've left Mel. She didn't want anyone with her. Back tomorrow as soon as I can and I'm having a chat with the DCI first to arrange to take control and get on with this. She's in a mess and has to go back to work on Monday. No real choice given the conditions at the moment. Maybe your Penny could give her a ring. All her mates seem to be in Manchester, and she didn't want to call anyone. I felt rotten leaving her on her own.*

Jordan handed over the phone to his wife and she scanned the text.

"I'll go over there tomorrow," she said. "I've got a couple of work things in the morning but should be finished by half eleven."

"Do you know the address?"

"Yes. I went to stay a couple of times when we were at uni. I reckon I can find it okay. The Old Roan, isn't it?"

Jordan tried to answer but the words were lost in a huge yawn.

"Come on, let's get off to bed." Penny held out a hand. "She'll be okay, won't she? Jean, I mean. I only met her twice, but she was lovely. She's just got herself upset with everything that's been happening. Lots of people are having trouble coping. I mean she's going to turn up, probably tomorrow, all embarrassed and sorry."

"I don't know, love. There are things I'm not happy about. Stella's in charge but I don't think she'll mind if I ask her to keep me in the loop. I'm going to see if I can be involved. We've got a thing going on at John Lennon. It's to do with mail theft and it's important but I'm sure Dave'll be able to swing it. We did that last time and it worked out fine. Well, apart from Stella getting herself kidnapped. By next week I should be able to give her more time. Once we have this court case all wrapped."

"Thanks, love. I know Stella's great but with the two of you working together it'll be sorted in no time."

As he turned to switch off the light Jordan sighed. He didn't think this was going to be anything like as easy as Penny thought. Many people had struggled through recent times and Jean Barker could easily join the number of people who just didn't make it. He shook the thought aside. She might well turn up in a day or two, shaken and embarrassed. He wasn't convinced.

Chapter 10

Jean remembered being woken by a noise on the side path. The cats were fighting again. The tom from next door must have been trying to get in through the cat flap. She went downstairs and opened the back door. Percy shot past her and slithered under the pan stand, where he cowered, yowling. It was a strange croaking growl full of fear and anger. She bent down to find out what was wrong. He wouldn't come out and she knelt on the cold floor reaching towards him and murmuring reassurance. There was a cold draught from the open door, and she shook her head at the ridiculous situation.

As her legs shot from under her, her chin hit the tiles with a thud that sent sparks behind her eyes. She tried to roll over but was held tight around the ankles. Someone grabbed her arms and dragged her hands behind her. It was the stuff of nightmares. She screamed.

The cat fled, his claws scratching and skidding against the floor. The intruder pulled Jean backwards using a handful of hair and then dragged something over her head. It smelled of earth and was rough against her skin. She panicked and gasped, squirming and twisting, kicking out with her feet, but the fabric sucked into her mouth, dirty and suffocating.

They still held on to her, pushing her down and sitting on her legs. The weight pressing her knees into the tiles was agony. Her ankles were tied. She tried to scream again, and her head was dragged up and slammed down onto the kitchen floor. She felt a tooth crack and blood from her split lip filled her mouth with the taste of metal. Now, with hands under her armpits she was dragged along the floor and outside. Her bare heels banged down the hard concrete of the steps. She twisted and pulled and heard a curse as the fiend stumbled. A plant pot fell and broke. When she tried again to yell out her head was smashed against the door frame.

She fought against the darkness. If she lost consciousness, she would be beaten. There wasn't enough power left in her legs to prevent herself being dragged along the side path.

Blood trickled from her mouth, mixing with the tears. There was no fight left. The strength had gone. She was bundled into a vehicle which bumped and bruised her already battered body as it took her away.

Now, she didn't know how much later it was. Her feet were restrained, and her hands fastened in front. The worst of it was the thing around her neck. It was heavy and hard, digging into the soft skin. He had fastened that onto her before taking the sack from her head. As her eyes adjusted to the low light, she saw the chain. It was attached to a ring on the wall and then snaked over her legs and up the front of her body. She had been able to reach it, to feel it with her fingers, but she couldn't stretch behind to where the collar was fastened. Her heels stung and her shoulders screamed in pain as she moved. On the side of her head the hair was matted and stiff, and her fingers, when she touched it, came away damp and sticky.

He came out of the darkness and leaned beside her to mutter quietly as he checked that she was secure.

"Don't worry," he told her. "It'll be alright."

The tickle of warm breath on the side of her face made her shudder and she tried to draw back. Her heart raced.

She begged him to let her go. She cried and promised that she would never tell anyone. It made no difference. She threatened him, lifting her chin, trying to seem unafraid. Her daughter would soon be looking for her, she said. He wouldn't get away with this. He stood over her and tipped his head to one side as he peered at her from behind the balaclava.

"I'll bring you some water. Try not to worry."

With that he had turned and walked out of the room. She heard the rattle of a lock and the slap of his shoes as he left.

Chapter 11

Jordan slid out from under the covers and went quietly into Harry's room. His son was sitting in his cot, chewing on the ear of a pink fluffy cat.

"Morning, mate."

He lifted the boy and carried him down to the kitchen. He put on a pot of coffee and scanned the messages on his phone.

'Morning,' Stella had posted. 'On my way in. Going to try and get back to Old Roan later. Everything's in place now for a bit of a media blitz so I need a word with Mel Barker. Speak later.'

Jordan pursed his lips. Someone whom Penny knew was involved in this and that was chilling. The horrors that he saw in his work always moved him, appalled him, and angered him, but they were at arm's length. Usually. This was all a bit close to home.

It was still very early but there was a lot to do. He needed to get to St Anne Street and take care of business there. He'd have a word with his immediate boss. If possible, he would like to give his attention to Jean and Mel. To do that he would probably need to relocate to Copy Lane. That would require some organisation and careful handling by David Griffiths. He didn't want to step on any toes, but time was already running out for Mel's mum. The first forty-eight hours were always the most important. So much of that had already been lost.

He grabbed an energy bar and slid it into his jacket pocket, gathered up his son, and went back to the bedroom where Penny was beginning to stir.

"I'm off, love. I want to get an early start," he said. "Coffee's made."

"Right, right. I'm awake. Is there any news?"

Jordan shook his head.

"I'll go over there as soon as I get out of the office," Penny said.

"Great. You might well meet Stella over there. I'll try and come by when I get out of court."

Penny's eyes filled with tears.

"Poor Jean. She will be alright, won't she?"

There was no answer. They both knew anything he said now was simply whistling in the dark. He bent and kissed his wife and boy.

"Later, love."

The morning was damp and grey with no promise of sun. Jordan pulled out of the drive and into the quiet Crosby streets. Deep in his belly he had the terrible feeling that this tragedy was already being played out. He shook his head, tried to move the thoughts away. They would throw everything they had at the search for the missing woman. The trouble was that with personnel shortages and lack of funding, what they had was so very little.

Chapter 12

Penny was distracted and anxious and in the end cut her shift at Citizens Advice short. Memories flooded back as she drove through Aintree to where Jean lived.

In the house, Mel looked haggard and worn. There were dark rings under her eyes. It was obvious she'd hardly slept. Penny wrapped her arms around her friend's shoulders, and they sat together beside the table.

"I was just bringing Mel up to date," said Stella. "We've sent out an alert to all the ports and airports. We've got the CCTV footage from Lime Street Station to review, and we've been scanning the stuff from the motorway service areas in both directions. Apart from that I've been in touch with the press section. We're going to get an appeal out as soon as we can. We've been looking for a picture of Jean. I think we are going for one from Mel's phone. It's the most recent."

Mel held the mobile out for Penny to see.

"It's a few months old now. This was in Manchester when she came up for the weekend."

"She hasn't changed a bit from when I remember her."

"No, she doesn't ever seem to. Her hair might be a bit greyer, a bit thinner, I suppose. But she's lucky, she has lovely skin – no wrinkles. She looks a lot younger than she is and she keeps fit. Oh Jesus, Penny. I can't bear this. Where is she?"

Penny squeezed her hand. "It'll be alright. She's probably just thrown a bit of a wobbler and maybe needed to get away for a bit."

Mel shook her head. "No, it's no good. She just wouldn't. She knew I was coming down. She was really looking forward to it."

"Mel," Penny said, "I know your mum looks well in this picture but, how old is she now?"

"She's just turned sixty-nine."

"You're right, she doesn't look it. But is she well? Mentally, you know. Has she been forgetting things? Has she been confused at all?"

"Confused?" Mel said.

"Yeah, she's not that old but she lost your dad and then there's been all this other mess. You know depression can cause people to become a bit low, a bit confused and…"

"She hasn't got dementia if that's what you're getting at. Shit, Pens. I'm a nurse. I worked in an elderly care unit for two years. I'd have known. There was nothing. No, she hasn't just gone off and forgotten who she is or where she should be. No. Something horrible has happened to her. I just know it. I'm supposed to be back in work on Monday. How the hell can I go back now? How can I be anywhere but here?"

"Don't get upset, love."

As she spoke, Penny knew that the words were hollow and there was nothing that would help Mel. She was in a pit of despair and there was just one way that she would come out of it.

"Come on, Mel. Let's get that picture to the press section so they can get it out to the television and the papers. Sitting here going over stuff isn't helping any of us," Stella said.

Chapter 13

Jean hadn't slept. How could she sleep? It was cold in this room. It was dark. On one wall there was a square panel which could have been a window, but it was covered with something. She wasn't close enough to see what it was, but it kept out all the light except for a small gap in one corner. It looked as though a piece of the covering had been scratched or torn away and by watching this Jean could see as the light changed. It was morning.

"It's Friday," she said aloud. "It's Friday and Mel will be home. She'll be looking for me."

She took in a deep breath and shouted into the dim room.

"My daughter will be looking for me. You have to let me go. I'll not tell anyone what you did but you have to let me go. I don't know what you want from me. I don't have anything. I'm not rich. What do you want?"

There was only the heavy quiet. Not quite silence. She could hear a bird. A blackbird, she thought. She heard cars, now and again. She had heard rain in the night.

From beyond the door she heard footsteps. Then came the rattle of the lock. Jean pushed herself backwards and straightened her aching back against the wall. She shuddered with fear. Her throat was dry, and her head ached, but she would meet this nightmare with her eyes open and her shoulders squared.

He pushed open the door and she saw, beyond him, a narrow hallway. It was lit by a single light in the ceiling. He turned and bent to the floor to retrieve a small square tray. She wasn't surprised that he wore a balaclava, she would have been more surprised if he had shown his face. Didn't they say in the films that if you saw their face, it meant they were going to kill you? So that was good, she didn't want to see his face.

"Good morning. I brought you brekkie. I don't suppose you slept much but don't worry. You'll get used to things soon enough and if you're good we can make you more comfortable. Here we are."

He put the tray on the floor beside her. She wanted to kick out at it, send it spinning across the room, but there was a bottle of water, and she wanted the water. There was a pastry of some sort wrapped in cellophane. There was an apple. He backed away quickly.

"You'll be able to reach from there. You have a nice breakfast. Bon appétit." He sniggered.

He had a local accent, but she had the feeling he was being careful with the way he spoke. It didn't sound natural, as if he was choosing the words carefully and trying not to be too Scouse.

"My hands are tied," Jean said.

"Oh I know, it'll be tricky for you, but I'm sure you can manage. It's just a little bit of rope."

"Let me go. I don't want breakfast. I want to go home. Just let me go. Leave me somewhere, anywhere and I'll find my way. What have I ever done to you? Who the hell are you anyway? Just let me go."

He shook his head, just once and tutted. He turned and walked out of the room. She heard the locks. She heard his footsteps walking away.

She needed to know whether he was still there, still in the building. She listened for the sound of a door closing. There was nothing. She listened for the sound of a car, there was nothing. So, did that mean he was still here? Was he just on the other side of the door in the dim corridor or in a room just beyond?

"Hello. Are you there? Please come back. Let's talk. Let's try and sort this out." There was nothing.

She reached out for the bottle of water. He was right about her hands. She could just about manage. How did he know that?

She pulled open the top. After a couple of big gulps she stopped. She didn't know how long it would be before there would be any more to drink. She should save some. Apart from anything else she had no toilet. It was inevitable that she would have to deal with that at some stage but maybe if she could hold off long enough, he would come back. Maybe he would let her go to a bathroom.

She pulled open the packet of a blueberry muffin and broke it into small pieces. It was dry but she chewed and swallowed. She had to be strong. She had to be strong for Mel and for herself. She had to stay strong enough to get out of this. She bit into the apple and winced at the pressure on her broken tooth. As she chewed carefully the room was suddenly and violently lit. High in two of the corners were spotlights. She was blinded for a moment and closed her eyes to shut out the glare. Then after a few minutes and just as suddenly, the light went out leaving her in the gloom, wondering what that could mean.

Chapter 14

Jordan walked away from the court room accompanied by David Griffiths.

"So, that went fairly well," Jordan said.

"Not bad. I still think we missed some of the top nobs, but we'll keep on trying. At least we've got a few scallies off the streets for a few years and more importantly got some of those poor women back home where they belong. We will have access to the scum we've put away today, so we'll pump for more information. It's not over until it's over. They call it people trafficking but really it's slavery, that's what it is. Just as bad as any other slavery." He pointed up to one of the beautiful stone buildings. "Ironic, isn't it?"

"The Town Hall?" Jordan said.

"Built by the proceeds of slavery. Have a close look sometime at the stonework, there and on many of the other grand buildings. All slavery and it's still going on. Nothing gets any better. It's bloody hopeless."

"We can only do what we can do, boss. We can only keep on trying. Listen, can I ask? Have you given any more thought to the missing woman? I know we've got the John Lennon thing still ongoing, but I reckon I can handle both. I feel a bit connected with Jean Barker's case. The daughter's a friend of Penny's."

"Yeah. You said. You can't be doing this too often, Jordan. Either you have to be fully committed to Serious and Organised or maybe we need to have another look at things."

"Oh, I do know. I know this is the second time I've asked to be seconded, but we've handled a lot of other stuff in between and I wouldn't be asking if it wasn't for Penny being friends with Mel."

"That's another thing, isn't it? Maybe you're too involved."

"No. No, I don't think so – not at all. I don't know either her or her mother, never met the mother."

"Okay, look. I'll clear it, but if things start to move on the mail theft investigation you have to drop it, so make sure that er… what's her name?"

"Stella, DS May."

"Yeah, her. Make sure she's able to take over if you have to do a runner. Now a quick pint and a pie, okay? We have got a small victory to celebrate today."

"Absolutely. Thanks, Dave."

"Good luck with the missing persons. Doesn't sound too good from what you've told me. You don't really know how long she's been gone, do you?"

"Not accurately, no."

The DCI raised his eyebrows and pursed his lips. Jordan knew that he was thinking the same as himself. Either Jean had run away for reasons they weren't yet aware of, or they were facing a grim discovery in a deserted spot and heartbreak for the family.

* * *

As Jordan drove to the outskirts of the city David Griffiths' words replayed in his head. He had been flattered and pleased when he was offered promotion to the specialist division, but if he drilled down to the honest part of himself it wasn't working out the way that he had hoped.

Yes, he gave it everything he could, stayed late, spent time away from the family chasing the gangs of people traffickers, the weapons smugglers, drug gangs, and this group that they were stalking now stealing from the mail bags at all the major airports. But so much of it was paper-shifting. There was a lot of liaising with other forces, which he didn't mind, but often their own part in an operation was small in comparison with others'.

There were the sweeps, the rounding up of low-lifes and the very satisfying arrests of the high-level criminals getting rich on the misery of others and the vile actions of the lower ranks. But honestly, he missed the immediacy of more local crime. He missed the satisfaction of helping members of the public on a one-to-one basis and had felt for a while that Serious and Organised was not where he wanted to be. There was the added consideration that he would probably have to wait for quite a while before there was any chance of promotion, unless he was ready to move, probably back to London. That wouldn't be all bad, his family were mostly still there, his mum and Nana Gloria, the two women who had brought him up. He didn't want London though, he liked Merseyside. He liked the people, and he liked the city.

As he drew up outside Jean Barker's house, he acknowledged it was probably time to have a heart-to-heart with Penny about what they wanted for themselves and Harry.

Chapter 15

"Hey, look at you all gussied up," Stella said as Jordan opened the door to the incident room. She pursed her lips and raised her eyebrows as she looked him up and down.

"Been in court this morning. Didn't have time to go home and change."

She was joking, of course she was, but he was uncomfortable now in his suit and tie. Some of the officers at desks close by were grinning as they peered at the screens.

"Well, it's good to see you anyway," she said. "Do you want coffee?"

"No, just had lunch, thanks. How are things shaping up?"

He didn't want to come across as standoffish, but the other staff didn't know him, and they probably didn't know the history between him and DS May. It didn't take much to start rumours and neither of them would benefit from that. He wanted to take his tie off but thought it might look too obvious now. He cleared his throat.

"Okay, everybody," Stella said, addressing the room. "This here is DI Carr. Some of you may know him. He's based in St Anne Street, down where the clever sods are, but he's going to give us a hand with the search for Jean Barker. Full disclosure, DI Carr's wife is a friend of Mel Barker. DI Carr–"

"Call me Jordan."

"Okay. Great. Jordan doesn't know either of them personally, but he was the one who reported Jean missing. So this is no reflection on us lot here and what we've been doing. It's just another head to try and solve this before it all goes bad."

"Are you going to be involved with the other case – the woman in the water, sir?" one of the civilians asked.

Jordan had to consider his response. He didn't want them to think he was being brought in over Stella's head.

"I'm just here to help in any way I can, but mainly I want to try and find Jean Barker as quickly as possible."

They were standing in front of Stella's desk now.

"Do you want to use that computer, Jordan?" Stella pointed to another workstation.

"Yep, anything."

The rest of the staff had gone back to work. There were a few raised eyebrows and side glances, but nobody seemed particularly put out.

"Listen, I've cleared it with David Griffiths for me to hang out here," Jordan said, "but it's possible I might have to cut and run if there are any developments in the big thing he's focused on right now."

"Okay. Better get on with things then. Just to get you up to speed. We've got a notice in the *Echo* today, online and in hard copy. We've got a bit on *Look North* and posts on the websites of all the forces. HOLMES has been updated. If she's walking around confused or whatever, we might have a chance. I've had Kath and Vi" – she waved a hand to two desks in the corner – "scanning CCTV of the buses into town from Old Roan. There is no sign of her at the station there and we looked at the ones either side. We've watched all the footage from Tuesday and Wednesday. We did pick her up at Asda on Tuesday morning, that was when the neighbour says she did shopping – yeah?"

Jordan nodded.

"She seemed to be alone, and nothing looked odd."

"Perhaps I could have a look at that? I've never met her. It'd be good to see her. After that I thought I'd go back to see Mel."

"She's not doing too well. She's absolutely torn. The plan originally was for her to be heading back to Manchester tomorrow ready for her next shift early Monday. The way things are in the hospitals at the moment she feels that she can't let them down. Poor thing is in a shocking state. How well does Penny know her?" Stella asked.

"They've been friends for a long time but they've not been as close since they left uni."

"I just wondered if you'd be able to have her stay with you? Am I out of order asking? You can say if I am. Only it'd be a help. I'd like to get the CSI team into the house. I would have liked to have done it sooner but I didn't have the heart to ask her to go and I can't really do it with her there. I did ask her to keep out of her mam's room and the lounge but that must be horrible for her. We'd already been in the kitchen anyway. If you can't, I understand, and we'll just have to try and get her back to Manchester more quickly."

"No, no – I'll ring Penny now, and then I'll take her back with me. Always providing she agrees of course," Jordan said.

"Brill. Erm, we will need her prints, just in case this goes nasty. Could you be a mate and arrange that for me as well?"

"Of course, anything that'll help. I'll take her to my house now, then come back here. Will you be staying here?"

"God yeah! I've got this other thing on, and we haven't been able to find where she came from yet either. Oh there is one thing. I'm going in the morning to have a word with the yoga teacher. It seems it's the only thing Jean Barker had been doing. They used to all get together in some hall but when the virus hit, they did online meetings. Then the teacher went on some sort of a retreat but she's back tomorrow. I just thought she might be able to give us an idea about who Jean was friendly with lately and her take on her mental state. Do you want to come with?"

"Yes, please. Okay, I'll head out now to Aintree and see you in about an hour or so. It's good to be working with you again, Stella."

"Same goes. Laters."

Chapter 16

The day had seemed endless. Now it slipped slowly into darkness, and nobody came. Jean had drunk the water and there was nothing left to eat. She had cried constantly. She had pulled at the bindings on her legs but all that did was to make her fingers bleed, and her ankles were bruised and aching.

She had called out over and over but if anyone heard they didn't come. For a while she had thumped her legs and feet on the floor. She had rattled the chain that snaked up the front of her body to her neck and her body was now sore everywhere. Her throat was on fire and her eyes felt like they were filled with sand.

The only change was the unwelcome one of sudden, glaring light. Unexpectedly and unexplained the room would be thrown into shocking illumination which lasted sometimes for just a few short minutes and sometimes for longer. She preferred the darkness. In the darkness she didn't need to see the bare walls and the stained and grubby floor. In the darkness she could close her eyes and pray for sleep.

When the footsteps came near she drew in a breath and held it. The rattle of the locks caused her heart to race and her stomach to turn. All day she had wanted someone, anyone, to come and now, now when it was happening, she was terrified.

She scuttled backwards on her behind and pulled her knees up to her chest. She closed her eyes. The door scraped across the gritty floor. She peered under her lids to see the dim light in the passageway beyond, and his soft shoes, and the twin pillars of his denim-clad legs. She waited in silence.

"Jean. I'm sorry, I didn't mean to leave you so long. Things came up. I've brought a couple of things to make you more comfortable."

"What do you mean?"

In response he rattled a bucket he held in one hand. He showed her a roll of toilet tissue. "I'll put them down here. You should be able to reach okay."

She had held on as long as possible but the inevitable had happened and she felt soiled and uncomfortable. "No, please let me go out. I promise I won't run or anything.

Just let me go to a proper toilet. You can tie me up again afterwards. I won't struggle."

"Now, now. Come on, this is not going to get you anywhere. Here, look what else I brought. That's a clever blanket with a plastic back. Wonderful what you can get nowadays. That'll be more comfortable."

"Untie me, please. Just untie my ankles. I promise I won't move. I won't struggle. Only don't leave me like this."

"In a little while. If you're good, I'll come back. But you have to promise me you'll stop all this shouting, all this silly noise. If you can be quiet, stay calm, then I'll bring you something nice to eat. Maybe I'll bring a pillow. We'll see. Now, how do you feel about that?"

"Please let me go. Please."

He sighed, pushing air through his nostrils in a snort. "Jean, Jean. Just be quiet for a bit. Sit still here and afterwards you can have something to eat, a nice drink. Would you like a nice cup of tea? I bet you would. All you have to do is sit quietly. Can you do that?"

"Yes, yes. I will. Please bring me a drink."

"Alright. One hour, Jean, just one little hour and then I'll come back."

He was gone. The room was dark again, the door closed, and all she heard was the faint noise of the world, far, far away, and all she could do was wait and hope and try not to cry. How did he know her name? The thought came to her that maybe she knew him. She tried to focus on the men that she had met. It wasn't a friend of her husband, it couldn't be. They didn't come round anymore but she would know if it was one of them. So, maybe someone from a shop or from the garage.

Her head was aching again, and she had to be quiet; she couldn't cry. She wanted him to bring her something to drink. She closed her eyes and tried to shut it all out.

Chapter 17

Stella was already in the incident room at Copy Lane the next morning when Jordan arrived armed with takeaway coffee and a bag of donuts.

"Cool. I remember this from last time. You and your coffee," Stella said.

"Well, I wasn't sure what sort of a set-up you had. I couldn't face a cup of instant this early."

"Cheeky sod, although I'll admit, all we have is instant – but it's not cheapo. I do have some standards. How's Mel?"

"She was still asleep when I left home. There were tears last night and she's pretty much decided that she's got to go back to work. She was talking to staff at the hospital and they're desperate. I've promised that we'll keep her up to date with everything we're doing and, of course, any developments."

Stella nodded. "It's all we can do for now and I think that maybe she's better off working. I do understand how she feels. I'd go mad if this was my mam."

"How are the family?" Jordan asked.

"Yeah, doing okay. Granda had his hip replaced and it was brilliant. He went private and he was spoiled rotten."

"Nice. Lucky he had insurance then?"

"Erm, well no. I paid for it. Listen, I'm just going to say this and then it's out there. I would really appreciate if you kept schtum. I know I can trust you." She paused and looked him directly in the eyes. "I can trust you, can't I?"

"Of course."

"Well, round about the time we were working together in Kirkby I had a bit of luck. We were slap bang in the middle of that case, so I didn't say anything. But. Well to put it bluntly I won a couple of million on the lottery."

"You didn't?"

"Yep. I did. I didn't want anyone to know because…" Stella shrugged, she had blushed and glanced away. "Well I didn't want people to treat me different and I knew they would. So, I never said anything. It was one of the reasons I left Kirkby when I did. I mean, I tried really hard not to let on, but… new car, Granda's operation, my house, and I bought a flat for my brother and his girlfriend. I'm buying another house for my mam, but she's being dead picky so it's taking ages. People notice stuff, don't they? So I thought, come to a new station and it'll all be different staff and that."

"Ha. Then I turned up."

"Oh God, no I didn't mean that. No, I'm chuffed to see you. Dead thrilled to be working with you again. Anyway, a lot of it's gone already. You think it's loads, don't you? It was actually just about four million and you think – shit, I'll never spend that. But you do. A new car, the properties. Mind, there's a lot invested. I just leave that to the bank, I haven't got the time to see advisors and whatnot about it. But it does mean I don't have to worry about treating myself and having a holiday. Ha! When I get time off."

"I am absolutely delighted for you. I really am. Wow, I've never known a millionaire before. Can I touch you for luck?"

"Oh go on then," Stella said, and she laughed and leaned forward.

Jordan reached over to put his hand on her shoulder. The door opened and two uniformed constables walked in. Jordan jerked backwards, but they'd seen. One of them grinned and winked at Jordan. He knew better than to respond so he picked up his coffee and turned to his workstation. Stella went to update notes on the whiteboard, but he could see the fierce colour creeping up her neck.

Chapter 18

The yoga teacher was thin, heading towards skinny. A middle-aged woman. When she opened the door, she was wearing a dark pink, loose, leisure suit and a shawl draped around her shoulders. Her long brown hair was tied back in a saggy ponytail. A pair of glasses were pushed onto the top of her head. Her wrist was ringed with several multicoloured, plaited bracelets. The nails on her bare feet were painted pink and she wore rings on two of her toes. She smiled and performed a namaste before she stood back to let them into the little semi.

Inside the house everything was clean, the walls were painted in shades of peach and magnolia, and the curtains were light voile that moved slightly in the breeze through the open window. A thin spiral of smoke from an incense burner perfumed the air. A chocolate point Siamese cat glared at them as they walked into the kitchen. With a stretch and one backward glance it slid through the cat flap into the garden.

"Don't mind Truffle, she's very antisocial. Would you like tea? I have herbal. Or coffee – decaf."

"We're fine thank you," Jordan said. "We don't want to keep you."

"It's okay. I'm just back from a lovely restful few days so I won't be wound up and anxious for a while yet."

She laughed self-deprecatingly then waved a hand in the direction of a settee and chair as she settled herself on a stool, feet flat on the floor and her hands folded in her lap.

"As I told you on the phone," Stella began, "Mrs Barker, Jean, hasn't been seen for a few days. We are now at the stage where we are concerned for her wellbeing. It would be helpful if you could tell us anything you know about Jean. The people she mixes with, your impression of her mood recently – anything really that comes to mind."

Veronica Surr leaned back in the chair and closed her eyes, she hummed under her breath. Jordan glanced at Stella who smirked. He grinned back.

"So, Jean had been coming to the lessons for just over two years. I think it was for the social side of things as much as the exercise and mindfulness. She is pleasant. Quiet really, but I think now and again she met one or two of the women for coffee afterwards and sometimes they went to the pub. I don't recommend it. They should go home and quietly enjoy the benefits of the classes but…" She shrugged and smiled. "Anyway, when the pandemic came along and the shutdowns, I did lessons on Zoom. It worked reasonably well. Some people didn't like it and after a while they fell away. Jean stayed with it. I think now and then she was lonely but coped as well as anyone with it all."

"So, you wouldn't have said she was depressed?" Jordan asked.

She shook her head. "You never really know, do you? But if she was, she hid it well."

"Can you give us a list of the women who attended the classes?" Stella said.

"Just the women?"

"Oh, I thought it would be only women"

"No, we have a couple of men. There's David Cooper and Sean Lamont. They've both been coming for ages."

"And was Jean Barker friendly with them?" Jordan asked.

"No more than anyone else. Is that you making assumptions, Detective Inspector?"

"No, but it's me being realistic."

This woman was beginning to get on Jordan's nerves. He'd had enough of the performance and had also spotted the bottle of gin in the kitchen cupboard and the pack of Yorkshire Tea behind the bread bin.

"I'll print it out for you next time I'm at the hall. I don't have a printer here. In the meantime, I could send you an electronic copy."

"That'd be great, thanks," Stella said. "So, are you going back to the actual physical classes now?"

"Yes, we are starting up next week. That's at the community centre. I'll be glad to get back there, it's best face to face. The Zoom has been okay but it's not the same. The poor hall has been all locked up. Just the caretaker going in to check on it and run the mop around. It's awful. We use the assembly hall just down the road. It's right next to the school. All part and parcel, really, shared grounds and all of that. You'd be very welcome to come along."

"Oh no, I don't think that's for me," Stella said. "I'm thinking of starting boxing or maybe taekwondo."

* * *

They left Veronica Surr to her mindfulness and, Jordan imagined, a nice strong cup of builder's tea.

"Is that right?" Jordan asked as they walked back to the car.

"What's that?"

"Boxing? Are you going to start boxing?"

"No, of course not, but she was really getting on my tits. Did you notice the ashtray on the table?"

Jordan gave a spurt of laughter. "Yes, I did, maybe Truffles likes a smoke now and again. Ah she's sent through the list of attendees. We need to have a word with them."

"Yes, how many?" Stella asked.

"Only about seven."

"Cool, we can start that today. Start with the men, yeah?"

"Is that you making assumptions, Detective Sergeant?"

"No, just me being realistic."

Stella grinned as she slid into her car and winked at Jordan.

Jordan leaned down to the window. "Back to Copy Lane?" he asked.

"Yes, I've got most of the team in doing overtime. We've been getting feedback from the publicity about Jean Barker. We could go through anything promising there and get someone to set up interviews with the yoga students. I guess Zoom or telephone will do as a start."

"Sounds good," Jordan said.

"Still nothing about my other woman. I think that maybe she came along the canal bank rather than on the road. There are no cameras down there, and I just don't know how wide to spread the search area. I've had a message to say the divers have come up empty-handed. No bag, no purse or anything – I suppose it was too much to hope for. They've wound it up, nothing to be gained from keeping on looking in the debris at the bottom. You wouldn't believe the stuff people throw in the water. They found an antique clock. They've dragged it out, I think Sergeant Philpot thinks it might be worth something and he never misses a chance."

"Bloody hell, who'd do that? Have you got her picture out?" Jordan said.

"I'm organising that now. I had to wait for a decent image as she didn't look so good straight out of the cut and then there was the post-mortem exam. Never an enhancement, are they? I'll chase the photographer because that's going to be my only hope now, I think."

"Okay, plenty to get on with. I'll see you back in the incident room."

Chapter 19

Following Stella's car along Altway, Jordan took a call from Penny at home.

"I just thought I'd let you know, love, I'm taking Mel to Lime Street in about an hour," she said. "She's got to get back to Manchester. They've called her from the hospital to say they are really struggling. She asked me to clear it with you and Stella."

"That's fine. Tell her that we'll keep her right up to date with everything and we're doing all that we can. How is she?"

"She's in pieces. I don't know how she can be expected to put in a shift in a high dependency unit considering the state she's in, but she's insisting she'll cope. I've told her that she can come back to stay with us any time. She's upstairs just now in the shower so I thought it was a good time to call you. Is there anything positive I can tell her?"

"Not really. We are just going through the routines. You could tell her that we have had some feedback from the publicity, but don't get her hopes up too much. I haven't had a chance to go through it yet. I'm on the way back now with Stella."

"Well, that's something anyway. Okay. I'll see you later. I'll probably go to my sister's after I've been to Lime Street."

"Yep. Great. I expect to be late. Don't wait up for me."

* * *

The incident room was busy. Notes had been added to the whiteboard and the staff were either on the phone or focused in on their screens.

There was the usual crop of hopeless and useless calls, but it was expected, and the experienced staff had correlated the reports cutting down on the number that Stella and Jordan had to review.

"Stella, have you seen this one?" Jordan picked up his tablet and carried it across the room.

The report was anonymous. The clerk who had taken the call had recorded a male – calm and clear but unwilling to give his name. He had seen a woman he thought was Jean Barker walking by the canal. She was on her own. He hadn't spoken to her. They played the call for everyone to listen to.

"Okay. It would have been helpful to talk to him," Stella said. "He was on a mobile with the number cloaked. I'll have a go at asking for a warrant to do a trace, but I don't think it'll go anywhere. It's a bit vague and it could be just someone wanting to be involved. Still, we need to make a note because it could be genuine and at least we would have an idea where she was on Thursday and from what was said she was well and on her own. We need to organise a second television piece and ask specifically for him to come forward. Did you all see the last one? They cut it for the PM's briefing. I reckon it was just too quick."

"On it." This from a young constable at a corner desk.

"Thanks. Speak to Sean in the press office, he'll know what to do. It's a little thing I know, but at least it's a thing." She turned to Jordan. "If you're ready. I reckon we have time for a quick bite and then maybe we can start on the yoga students." She turned back to the room. "Okay, guys, great work. We're taking a short break and I'd like a list of names and numbers for the yoga lot when we get back. Zooms if possible, if not then phone calls will do. Can someone organise that?"

"Happy to do that, Sergeant."

"Okay, did everyone get that – Constable…"

"Lewis."

"Thanks. Constable Lewis is in control of that stuff. Will someone get on to the photographer for our woman in the water? I need that ready before the *Echo* goes to print. When you speak to the press department can you give them a heads-up?"

"Yep. No probs," Lewis said.

"Not sure there's going to be much left in the canteen," Jordan said as they walked down the corridor. "Any suggestions?"

"There's the chippy just down the road. It's pretty good."

"Walking distance?"

"Quicker in the car."

They climbed into Jordan's car and headed out of the car park and down Copy Lane.

Chapter 20

Jean couldn't tell which part of her body hurt the most. Her head pounded and the various bruises and knocks ached constantly. Her tongue was sore where it had rubbed on the broken tooth and her eyes stung and watered.

Mentally she was exhausted. She had replayed the events over and over. Any idea of the passing of time was lost. For endless hours she sat in the dark. Now and again a sort of sleep took her away but never enough for her to feel rested and always she had to wake to this horror. Often it was the sudden light that woke her and each time it happened she waited in fear to see what it would mean but nothing would occur.

The man had been in and brought her a pair of soft trousers with an elastic waist. He snipped through the plastic binding her ankles and leapt away from her feet. He obviously thought that she still had the strength to fight. But all she wanted was to change into the clean trousers and curl herself back into a ball.

"There, that's nicer," he had crooned. "Look I brought you something to eat and when you've had that I'll have a lovely surprise for you. But that's later."

She had pleaded with him to let her go. She didn't believe it would do any good, but she had to try.

He ignored her and placed the paper bag holding a sausage roll on the floor.

He reached out and touched her hair. She pulled back with a hiss of fear. The man tutted quietly and then turned and left. She listened to the rattle of the locks and when she was certain that he wasn't coming back, she reached for the greasy bag. The lights flicked into life. She turned towards the corner to shield her eyes from the sudden brightness. She forced herself to chew and swallow the flakey pastry and over-seasoned stodgy meat product. She didn't want it, but she wanted the pain in her stomach and the nausea to go away and maybe the lukewarm snack would help.

He had left her a bottle of cold water and when she had gulped some of that, grease from the sausage roll coated her mouth and her sore tongue wouldn't let her clear it. Saliva rose in a flood, and she swallowed hard a couple of times. As her stomach settled, she curled back onto her side and closed her eyes. Shudders wracked her body. The lights went out and as she drifted into sleep quiet whimpers filled the silence.

In the top corner of the far wall a tiny red light was extinguished.

Chapter 21

Three Zooms and the rest were phone calls. All but one of the yoga students had been contacted and questioned. David Cooper was away working, according to his wife.

Jean was well liked but none of them counted her as a close friend. They didn't know much about her life save for what Stella and Jordan had already been told by Mel. She came to the classes, sometimes had a drink afterwards, and that was it.

"What about the ones who have left recently? Veronica said some members had drifted away when they went over to Zoom," Stella suggested.

Jordan shook his head. "It feels like a dead end. She really did keep herself to herself, didn't she? It's a bit sad to think of people like her during the worst of the lockdown."

"Yeah. It really showed some of the cracks in society, didn't it?" Stella said.

"Hmm, yes. I guess that's right but then it brought out the best in people as well. Not for Jean so much, I don't think. She did do the shopping for the next-door neighbour but didn't keep in touch with many people. Apart from her daughter she was on her own."

"Are you convinced she hasn't done a runner?" Stella asked.

"Well, aren't you?"

"Actually, I reckon so. There's no indication that she was depressed or upset. When you look at the video of her shopping, she looks quite cheerful. Not that you can tell that much behind the mask, but she chats with the cashier and acknowledges people in the car park."

"So, maybe she had some sort of other life that Mel and her yoga friends didn't know about. Have they finished going through her phone records?"

"Hold on a sec." Stella clicked her mouse and scrolled through the screen on her computer.

"Yes, the report is in. From a quick scan there's nothing much. They've gone back for a month to get us up and running. They're still doing it, but it'll have to wait its turn now. They're inundated in the forensic digital section, plus we don't even know if we've got a crime here, not for sure. Anyway, there are a couple of unknown numbers – the rest are in her contact list. She made calls to Mel, a couple to her neighbour and that's about it really. There are two numbers that seem to have been cold calls. One that they tracked back to the Red Cross and one trying to sell her a funeral plan. Bloody hell, she was practically a recluse. There has to be something though. We're being thick."

"We'll keep digging, Stella." As he spoke Jordan's phone burbled. "Sorry, it's Penny. I need to get this. Back in a minute."

Jordan wasn't gone long but as he walked back into the room Stella could tell the call hadn't been good news.

"Problem?"

He pursed his lips and blew out a puff of air. "Erm, I don't really know. Well, yes there's a problem. Nana Gloria."

"Oh right, your relatives in London."

"Yeah, my mum's mum. Helped to bring me up. She's special, important, you know."

"Okay. So…"

"That was Penny, they've rung to say Nana has been taken into hospital."

"Oh shit, mate. Do you know why?"

Jordan shook his head. Stella was embarrassed to see the glint of tears in his eyes. She stood and came around the desk.

"What are you going to do?"

"Right now there's nothing I can do. She's not allowed visitors. I don't even know where she is. Well, I know she's in hospital but at the moment she's just in the A&E. Oh, God. Thing is, I don't actually know what's wrong with her yet. My younger brother rang Penny just to let us know. He doesn't live with her. He just said that the ambulance had to be called early this morning. I hope she's not stuck in an ambulance waiting to be seen. You know, we've seen it on the news over and over, but you just don't think it'll be you. You don't think it'll come this close."

"Well, you don't know enough yet, do you? Come on, mate, get off home and see what you can find out. Just let me know what's happening and if you have to go down there, it'll be okay. We'll cope."

"Thanks, Stella, but I think I'll just stay here. Penny has gone to her sister's with Harry and there's nothing I can do. They all know how to contact me, and I'll just be driving myself mad in the house."

She acted instinctively and stepped forward. As she wrapped her arms round him to give him a hug the door opened, and DCI Martin walked into the room.

Chapter 22

"Everything okay here?" DCI Josh Martin stood at the door glancing from Jordan to Stella who had jerked backwards banging her leg on the edge of the desk.

"Yes, sir," Stella said.

"No, not really," Jordan said, their words colliding and falling over each other.

There was a tense silence.

"DI Carr had some bad news," Stella said.

"Okay. Sorry to hear that. Anything I can do, Jordan?"

"No, thank you, sir. Just a bit of a family emergency."

"Do you need leave?"

"Er, no. There's nothing I can do for the moment. Perhaps a couple of hours in the next few days."

"Okay, well let me know if things change."

"Yes, sir. Thank you."

"I just came down to see what movement there'd been on the woman in the canal."

"Sorry, sir. We haven't got anything really big. We've got a request for information out; we had to wait for a picture that was suitable for distribution. Nothing turned up from the divers or the house-to-house."

"Stalled a bit then?" the DCI said.

Stella lowered her gaze. There was nothing much she could say. She knew she was being judged and it was uncomfortable.

"Okay, well carry on. Let me know when I have something positive to feed back. There's some impatience higher up."

As he left Jordan turned and raised his eyebrows and Stella screwed her eyes tight shut and then grinned.

"Timing, eh?"

"Yeah," he said. "Not to worry. Listen, I know I'm here mainly about Jean, but I'm happy to pitch in with everything. Do you want me to go through the pictures and what you have about the other woman?"

They didn't have much, and it had all been seen before. After a frustrating few hours of going over it again, Stella said, "Oh, come on, let's call it a night. Back in the morning."

"Let's meet at the canal, early's okay. I don't reckon I'm going to get much sleep tonight anyway."

"Thanks, mate. I appreciate it. I hope you have good news from your mam. Do you fancy a drink? Or we could go to the offy and you know you're welcome back at mine. Of course it's a tip right now."

"No, it's fine. I think I'll just go home. Penny was planning on coming back later. Thank you anyway."

* * *

By the time his wife arrived, Jordan had seen the appeal on the local television for information on both of the cases. He gave it an hour before he called the station to speak to the late-shift officers and civilians answering the phones. They were fielding the expected spew of calls and trying to sort the rubbish from the potentially useful.

It was frustrating and sad and on top of everything else he was depressed and worried about his family. However, there was something niggling at the back of his mind that he couldn't quite grasp. He knew from experience that he had to just give it time, let it work itself forward. He pushed the laptop across the dining table and sighed.

"Are you okay, love?" Penny had put the baby in his cot and then poured a glass of wine for them both. "I know you're not. I know you're worried about Gloria, but you seem really low. She'll be okay, you know. She's tough."

"I hope so. I really hope so. But it's everything just now. Jean Barker, then a nasty murder, and we just don't seem to be getting anywhere."

"It's early days, isn't it? With Jean."

"It is but we need something. I need a light-bulb moment and my mind is just whirling with it all."

"Then we should have some cheese on toast, some whisky and get off to bed."

"You're right. Of course you are. Thanks, Penny."

"Don't be silly. It'll all be okay."

"I'll have to go in tomorrow, always providing there's nothing more from Mum."

"Of course you will, and I'll be here if they call. I'm going to work from home next week as well. We are still restricting person-to-person appointments where we can, so I've got a chance to catch up on paperwork. I'll hold the fort and if anything at all needs your attention, I'll let you know right away. Okay?"

Jordan wrapped his arms around his wife. "Okay. Come on, I'll do the toast."

Chapter 23

On the canal bank the towpath was muddy and disturbed. It had been wet overnight. Cyclists and joggers had churned up the earth. Jordan and Stella were under the Melling Road bridge watching the water dimple under steady rain.

"So, she was between the two bridges?" Jordan asked.

He swept his gaze back and forth from the railway crossing to the bridge on the A59.

"Yes. Not quite in the middle and the woman who pulled her out sort of hooked her using a tree limb that had been broken off. We took that away, but it didn't tell us anything. I thought that if she jumped in from the bridge then she'd be further away from the edge. I mean you would, wouldn't you?"

Jordan shrugged. "I don't know, depends on which direction she jumped. The canal water doesn't really move much. It doesn't actually flow. I suppose it does when the locks are opened and boats go past, but not normally."

"No, it's not like it's a river."

"So, where are the nearest locks?" Jordan asked.

"Let's have a look. My tablet is in the car."

It was warm and dry, and the car still had the new smell.

"This is nice," Jordan said as he settled back into the heated seat.

"Yeah, it's a couple of steps up from my old clanger."

"How the other half live, eh?"

He grinned as he said it, but Stella didn't respond. He sensed a tightening in her shoulders. So, she was still not comfortable with her new status.

"Sorry, just joking."

"Yeah, I know. Don't take no notice. I know I'm a divvy. It's just that all my life we've been – well what do they call it? – inverted snobs. '*Rich people are all knobs and not to be trusted and must be up to no good. But look at us – we're honest working class.*' I know it's all crap but it's how my family have always been. Especially Granda and my brother. Anyway, I just can't think of myself as rich."

"If it helps, I reckon you're exactly the same as when I first met you. Well, apart from the new car, of course," Jordan said.

She turned and smiled at him, and the awkwardness passed.

"Come on," she said, "let's get Google Earth up. The Canal and River Trust have a website as well. Hang on a minute."

They leaned together to study the small screen on Stella's tablet.

"Well, there are some down in the city," she said. "Down by Albert Dock. They've connected the canal there now. The Link, they call it. Looking at the map it's a sort of offshoot. So there's that."

"That's quite a long way, isn't it? And it's not a direct route so I don't think it could have had much impact. What about the other way?"

"Okay. There's a set of locks at Wigan, then there's another one at Rufford."

"Where's that?" Jordan asked.

"Appley Bridge. It's out near Burscough, by Ormskirk."

"Oh, okay I know Ormskirk. That's quite a long way from here, isn't it? It's too far. I'm sure it does make a difference but not enough to move a body. If that's the nearest, I just don't see it."

"Canal boats would move the water as they passed," she said. "There's plenty of them nowadays, it's really popular. But they'd see a body floating about and if they hit one it would have been beaten up more than our woman was."

"So she must have gone in near to where she was found. I guess that helps. You know the best thing here is to wait for the report from the dive team. I'm sure they've already covered all this."

"Yes, I'll be interested to see what they have to say."

They had come back to the bank and neither of them really knew why. As they gazed at the dark water the niggle at the back of Jordan's brain grew and formed.

"This is going to sound really a bit 'out there' but, you know the call we had about Jean Barker?"

"The bloke who said he'd seen her?" she said.

"Yes. Didn't he say he'd seen her walking by the canal?"

"Yes, he did. But the canal snakes all around this area. Surely you're not thinking there's anything in that. I mean there's no reason to think there's a connection, is there? That'd be a hell of a coincidence. I don't do coincidence, I reckon that's usually people trying to make things fit their ideas, mostly anyway. No offence and that."

"No. You're probably right," Jordan said. But the niggle wouldn't go away.

"What's the news from London anyway? How's your nan?" Stella asked.

"Yeah. Not as bad as it could have been. Apparently, Nana Gloria has had some sort of fibrillation attack. It's to do with her heart rhythm."

"So not the virus then?"

"No. Not that. They kept her in overnight to do some tests, but they reckon they can probably let her go home as soon as it's settled down. She'll need some follow-up and treatment, medication probably, but they are going to get her out of the hospital as soon as they can."

"Does she live on her tod?"

"She does, but her flat is really near my mum's. Mind, I think they are trying to arrange for her to go and stay with Mum. It's a relief."

"That's really brill. I'm dead made up for you. Okay, in that case, let's get back to the station and start going through the calls from the appeal yesterday."

"Okay. Tell you what. It's still early, let's walk up the towpath for a bit. The rain's stopped and we probably won't get much more fresh air today, not once we're back in the office. I don't think we'll find anything, it's already all been examined, but it's just sometimes helpful to be at the locus."

"Oh go on then. Hold on though. I need to change my shoes. Not wrecking these trainers, they're new."

Chapter 24

While he waited for Stella to change into boots Jordan called his brother. He was pushing his phone back into his jacket as she joined him.

"Everything okay?"

"Yes, nothing new. Still hoping they can send her home today. Are you ready? We'll just go up as far as the next bridge, yeah?"

There were still a couple of lengths of crime scene tape caught in the trees. The branches on the canal side shrubs were broken and bent in places. Here and there was evidence of what had happened. The rain lessened and the sky started to brighten. Ducks came out onto the water. A couple of early joggers passed, splashing through the puddles.

"We could do with questioning these joggers and cyclists," Jordan said. "They might have seen something that they didn't think was important."

"We did that on the first couple of days and there was nothing. Nobody saw anything out of the ordinary. Well, not until the dog walker's morning went to crap. Mind, have you watched them? They're so busy concentrating on not falling in or falling off that they don't look around."

"I should have known you'd have that covered already, sorry. Just trying to think it through, you know."

"It's fine. A new view on it all can't do any harm because I'm getting nowhere. It would probably be worth coming back on Thursday. You know, in case people have a weekly routine or what have you," Stella said.

"Well, I guess we're just wasting time right now. It's getting on for eight, we should head back. I wonder if we can pick up a bacon roll on the way?"

"I'm sure we can. Is it the smell that made you think of it?"

"Yes," he said, "I thought I was imagining it. My mouth's watering."

"No, I'm getting it as well. It must be from that."

Stella pointed to a narrowboat moored against the towpath. Ropes fore and aft were tied to stakes hammered into the soil. It wasn't a pretty-looking thing. The website had shown images of brightly painted barges trimmed with flags and flowers, but this was a plain, dark grey vessel. The cabin was built of plywood covered with a thin coat of paint. Faded curtains hung at the windows. A couple of tough polythene bags filled with logs had been thrown in the space at the fore, and a bike was tied to the roof with blue plastic rope. Aft in the transom there was an old wooden chair, the back of which had been mended with cord. The license stuck on the inside of the window was out of date by a couple of months. The smell of bacon wafting towards them was torment to Jordan and Stella, neither of whom had eaten.

"Hello," Jordan called out as he knocked with his knuckles on one of the windows.

The disturbance set a dog barking somewhere inside and there was a yell to quiet it. The small door at the end of the cabin was flung open.

"Bugger off. What the hell are you yelling at? Leave me in peace."

Jordan held up his warrant card. "Sorry to disturb you, sir. I wonder if we can have a quick word."

"No, you bloody can't. I've already spoken to a bugger in uniform days ago. Leave me in peace, I'm having my breakfast. I've nothing to say to you lot. I've done nothing wrong. Just get on your way. Stupid sods. Getting in the way of someone just trying to make a living."

With that he turned and slammed the door. They heard him inside shouting at the dog which continued to bark intermittently.

"Oh well, bacon baps it is then. Your shout, I reckon, under the circumstances and what have you," Jordan said.

Chapter 25

It was quiet back in the incident room. Early Sunday morning had seen most of the civilians on flexitime treating themselves to a lie-in. Lack of progress and the tedium of staring at CCTV and answering the phone with very little forward progress was taking its toll. A solitary figure sat at a desk in the corner of the room. He looked up as Stella and Jordan came in with their takeaway coffee and polystyrene boxes holding bacon rolls.

Stella's momentary embarrassment faded when she spotted the cardboard coffee mug on the desk and the greasy paper bag screwed into a ball beside it. Fair enough, he'd had his breakfast.

"DC Grice, isn't it?"

"Yes, Sergeant. John."

"The woman in the canal – can you go through the interviews and find one relating to a barge owner who was moored near to the railway bridge? He said he'd spoken to someone, and we'd like to have a look at his statement. Sorry I don't have his name, but the barge was called *Jayne* spelled with a 'y'."

"On it."

They sat at their own desks checking overnight reports. For a while there was quiet except for the clatter of a keyboard and the rustle of paper napkins.

"That was good." Jordan picked up the debris and headed for the door. "I'll stick it in the bin outside. We don't want to torment anyone coming in with left-over smell."

As Jordan took the rubbish outside, the young constable turned to Stella. "Sergeant, I think this might be what you're looking for. An interview with somebody called Billy Tranter. The officer who spoke to him reported he was pretty uncooperative. Been moored around the bridges for a couple of weeks. Denied seeing or hearing anyone or anything out of the ordinary until the disturbance after the body was found. He left that day in a bit of a huff apparently, cursing at the bobbies searching the bank. Came back next morning by all accounts. Told the guy on duty he'd come back because he had a casual job tidying a garden and he hadn't finished so hadn't been paid."

"Okay, I'll have a look at it. Send me a copy, will you?"

"I've done that. According to the report he didn't have anything to say of use and threw the copper off his boat pretty quickly."

"Hmm. Maybe I'll go and have another chat with him. Can you do a check just make sure he isn't known to us?"

Jordan re-entered the room to pick up his coat and laptop.

"Sorry, Stella, I need to go home, I think. Nana isn't being discharged. They're worried about her breathing. I need to be able to talk to the hospital and the family and I don't think it's right to be doing it here."

"No, course not. You shoot off, mate. Let me know what happens. I'm going to go back out to have a word with that boat bloke as soon as I've gone through the calls about Jean Barker's appeal."

"Stick at it, Stella. Something's gonna pop soon."

Chapter 26

Back at the canal, the narrowboat was moored in the same place. Alongside it the bike had been laid in the grass with a chain around the frame and handlebars and then attached to the mooring stake. On the barge was another sack of logs and a pile of green kindling. Obviously, Billy Tranter had been back to the garden work. If he had been paid his attitude may have mellowed.

She almost cried out 'Ahoy there'. Forever after she would be grateful for the fact that Tranter appeared in the fore well fiddling with a pipe and saved her that humiliation. He glared at her and carried on packing the bowl.

If this had been a house and she had no warrant, then the next stage would be clear. She would make a request to go inside and talk, which usually was granted, and if not, a dialogue on the doorstep was not so bad an option. Now, she didn't know what the protocol should be. She'd avoided the pirate speak but was she supposed to ask for permission to 'come aboard'? In the end she took the easy option.

"I need a word."

"Where's the boss?" Tranter glanced at Stella briefly and sniffed. He went back to the pipe, rooting in a small tin and tamping the leaves into the bowl. "The boss. Your guvnor – the bloke."

"My colleague's not here today. I'm in charge of this case and I want a word with you."

"In charge, a young lass. Bloody crackers. Don't want to waste my time talking to the monkey. Might talk to the organ grinder. Might, mind you. Might not."

"I can get a warrant to look over this thing. I can take you to the station to answer my questions. It's up to you."

"Or, you can get yourself away from my boat and leave me alone. Go on, get back to the kitchen where you belong. Stupid bitch."

He pulled a box of matches from his pocket and began to light the pipe. The smoke drifting towards her was fragrant and obviously not just tobacco.

"I could have you right now. I could take you in for what you've got in that. I know a moke when I smell one."

Tranter said nothing more. He slammed open the cabin door and let the dog out into the fore well where it began to bark. Stella didn't believe that it was a threat. The feathery tail was wagging and there was no growling. Nevertheless she wasn't going to take the risk of trying to climb onto the boat.

"I'll be back, Mr Tranter," she called out, "and I'll be bringing a warrant to have a look at your barge, and if this dog causes any trouble, you might find we'll be taking him away as a dangerous animal."

There was no response. She knew as she walked back along the towpath that she had made a mistake forewarning him of her plans. He would be gone, wouldn't he? Sod it. She called through to the station.

"I need a uniformed officer to come up to the canal by Old Roan. There's a barge here that I want to keep an eye on."

"Sorry, Detective Sargeant, I've nobody. There's been an accident on the motorway and there's an illegal party in Netherton. A crowd of kids in a warehouse; we have to shift them."

"What, nobody? Not even a special constable?"

"Sorry. Nobody. Too many off sick, and not enough to start with anyway."

"Bugger."

"Sorry."

There was nothing she could do, there was no point in hanging around. She would be better served spending her time obtaining a warrant to search the boat. At least he could only go up and down the canal, so they'd find him even if he was miles away. She couldn't see him leaving his boat and his dog.

As she walked back to the car, she heard the engine start and turned to see a small plume of dark smoke from the exhaust.

Chapter 27

Stella pulled onto the parking area in front of her flat in Aintree. The works were still in progress. It would be worth it with new soundproofing, the main room and kitchen of her own flat transformed into a modern open space, and a separate entrance for the apartment upstairs. However, the mess and muck were getting her down. She had considered moving out while it was going on but really packing up all her things and then bringing them back again afterwards seemed like too much work.

They had managed to enlarge the tarmacked path in the front of the house by chopping down some old gnarly shrubs and now both her and the neighbour upstairs were able to park off-street, providing neither of them bought a bigger car. Her neighbour was already home, and she would give him a knock later, see if he wanted a glass of wine. Something to take her mind off dead and missing women just for a short while. He always cheered her up and she knew she could depend on his discretion.

But before that, she needed to call Jordan.

"Hiya, mate. What's the news from London?"

"Well, it's not too bad. Her breathing issues seem to be because of the heart problems, and they can control it with medication."

"That's good."

"Yeah, maybe it is but I really want to hear that she's home. I want her away from the danger of picking up the virus while she's in hospital. Anyway, there's nothing for me to do right now. Sorry I left you in the lurch."

"Don't be daft. You had no choice – I get it. So, I went back to that bloke on the barge. His name is Tranter, Billy. He was charming and helpful. Made me tea and shortbread. We had a lovely chat. Oh no, wait – bloody misogynist prat. He wanted to speak to the organ grinder – that's you by the way."

"Oh."

"Yeah! Oh. Anyway, I'm not happy with him. He was moored there, and he must have heard something when that woman went into the water. Surely."

"You'd think."

"Although he might have been spaced out. He had the nerve to light up a pipe while I was there, and he wasn't smoking no baccy."

"So, what do you want to do?"

"I'm getting a warrant tomorrow and I'm going to pull that bloody boat to bits if necessary."

"Okay. Nothing more about Jean Barker?"

"I've spoken to Mel," she said. "That wasn't fun. She hasn't had any contact. I reckon it's pretty certain we're looking at something nasty by now and she knows it as well as I do. I'd still like a word with whoever it was who thought they saw her walking by the cut. We're going to get an appeal on *Crimewatch* but that's not until later in the week. I reckon we should speak to the one bloke from the yoga class that we haven't interviewed yet. I don't remember asking his missus how long the trip was planned. I wonder if there's anything to be read into that – him going away just now?"

"Not very likely, he's a rep for a pharma company but he also delivers urgent medication when necessary. I agree we need to see him though, and if he's not back yet we need more details."

"Apart from that there's nothing really. She's vanished. I'll get the team back on CCTV tomorrow and we'll widen the search, but we need some luck here, Jordan, and I hate that. It shouldn't be about luck, should it?"

"No, but sometimes it just is. Anyway, I'm in early tomorrow and we'll get on with it."

"Yep. Say hi to Penny for me."

"I will, and you try and get some rest."

Chapter 28

It felt like morning. There was a change in the light and somewhere there was a bird singing, it was the blackbird again. So sweet it made her eyes fill with tears. Jean rolled onto her back and groaned. When she had been younger, she had suffered from shingles and the pain had been horrendous. She always remembered how bad it felt. The labour when she delivered Mel had been tough and protracted. It was soon pushed into the background, as these things are, but it was still there in her memory. The way that she felt now, however, was worse than any of that.

She hurt all over. Her head pounded and every muscle and joint was agony. Her stomach growled and complained from lack of food. Her throat was raw from thirst, from crying and from calling out for help. No-one heard her, but every now and then she tried. Just in case.

When she managed cohesive thought, she tried to make sense of it all. At first, she had been sure that he would rape her. The few times that he had come into the room she had tried to prepare herself for the worst. She would fight with everything she had and would die if that was how it would be. It didn't happen and now she didn't think it would.

How could he even contemplate touching her? She stank and must look worse than she felt. So what was it for? She had no money. Mel had no money. There was no point at all in him considering a ransom. She didn't believe she'd ever hurt anyone. Not so badly to make them want to do this to her, and never deliberately.

On more than one occasion she had tried to make him talk. She had pleaded with him to tell her what it was about. She told him she would do anything just to make it right if he would only let her go. He didn't even respond to that but sighed and told her to relax and then everything would get better, and she would get used to it in time.

He had been in while she was lost in a stupor and left a small chocolate biscuit in a plastic wrapper and a bottle of water. She had eaten the Kit Kat and swigged most of the water, and used a little of it to wipe her face and clean the crud that had collected in the corners of her eyes.

She felt inhuman.

Dehydration tormented her with visions of rivers and pools. She would dive into them in her dreams only to wake with a start to cramp in her fingers and legs, and soreness of her skin.

She couldn't go on. She simply wanted this to be over. It had only been the thought of Mel that had made her struggle on, fighting to stay alert and alive. She had held to the hope that either he would just let her go or she would find a way to get out. There were no longer ties around her ankles, and her wrists had been freed, but no matter – she could do nothing about the metal collar around her neck.

She lay as flat as she could on the blanket on the cold floor and tried to relax her muscles. She had tried to remember the yoga meditations, the breathing exercises and the mantra, but the pain in every part of her body and the total despair made it impossible. It had taken such a short time to reduce her to this. She had thought she was fit but quickly the vision of herself as someone who was 'good for her age' and keeping it together was lost. Now she was nothing but an aging old bag with nothing to look forward to and with little time left.

She had let her mind wander back to the days before the lockdowns when she had gone to the classes, when she had gone to the library to borrow books and meet with the small reading group. She lost herself in the memory and it had seemed very real and for a while there had been some comfort. Now she'd had enough. It was over and she couldn't fight any more. She closed her eyes and thought of her daughter and sent her love out into the ether.

Chapter 29

The team were already in the office when Jordan arrived just after seven. On the whiteboard was a picture of the *Jayne* and a few notes regarding Billy Tranter, along with an old mug shot. As Jordan stripped off his leather jacket and popped the top on his coffee cup, Constable Grice pinned up a couple of sheets of paper.

Stella stood and waited for quiet.

"Okay, DC Grice – John. I think you all know him."

"Congratulations, mate." This from one of the civilians who raised a bottle of Coke in a toast.

"Thanks, Stew. Made it at last, eh?" Grice said.

"Yes, well, as he's now a detective, John put in a shift yesterday while you lot were all watching Netflix and playing GT Racing or whatever it is you do now," Stella said. "He's pulled out some information on a bloke who it appears lives on a canal barge. Billy Tranter. He's been done for small-time stuff. Shoplifting, selling weed from the boat, a couple of drunk and disorderlies, and affray. He's really just a scally and a no-mark. I'm going down with Jordan this morning and we're going to have a look round his barge. If we can find the bloody thing. I know he moved it yesterday, but we've got the mobile patrols alerted. It wasn't possible to get a warrant because all I had was him smoking weed and a bad feeling which wasn't considered urgent enough to bother a magistrate on a Sunday."

There was a low-level groan in the room.

"DCI Martin pulled some strings today and we have one now. Those vessels don't travel all that fast so he can't have got very far."

"Is he a person of interest then?" a clerk asked.

"Not officially but I didn't like his attitude and that was enough to make me want to annoy him." There was a ripple of laughter. "No, seriously, he's an unpleasant individual and if he was there when the woman went in the water, he knows something. Our priority is to identify her. So back on the computers today and follow up any misper reports. I reckon we should go back a bit further. Don't forget she could have changed her appearance quite a lot if she's been adrift for a while. Let's extend it from six months to a year. Anything that looks likely. On that, I think Jordan has an idea."

"Thanks, Stella. We need one of you to get in touch with Border Force. John, can I leave that with you? We don't know that she's foreign but in the absence of any other information then we have to look at the possibility. I don't even want to consider that she was trafficked yet because that opens a whole new can of worms. Also" – he turned to Stella who gave a nod – "it's a long shot but there seems to me that there could be a link between her and Jean Barker's disappearance. It's tenuous at best but Mrs Barker was seen walking by the canal not all that long after this woman turned up there. I may be clutching at straws but it's two events in the same location. One unknown woman turning up dead and one woman vanishing. Unlikely events both of them, and both on our patch. So, it might just be that the bloke who saw Jean Barker has seen other things. There is a reason he didn't give his name. What was he doing there on a wet day? He could be a total innocent but let's find out." He shrugged. "I'm afraid it means just more viewing of the CCTV. I know it's tedious, but it pays dividends over and over so stick at it – thanks, Stella."

"Right get on with it. Find me something, anything. We'll be down by the canal for a bit now hopefully having a chat with Mr Tranter. We're arranging another appeal and hopefully this one won't be cut short to make way for announcements by the Prime Minister. I know these things are important, but they could have organised things better on *Look North*. Nothing we can do about it, so we just have to go again and that'll mean more phone calls," Stella said.

They ignored the groans as they left. Jordan held the door and was aware of a low whistle from the group in the room as Stella nodded and thanked him.

"Plonkers," he muttered.

Chapter 30

Jean heard the approach of footsteps. She felt the change of air as the door opened. A strip of light from the corridor speared across the dirty floor. She couldn't be bothered to move. She was disappointed to find she had survived another night. She had closed her eyes a few hours ago and wished it was the last time. Although she had shed tears for Mel, she didn't want to face another day, another hour of this torment.

"Come on, lazybones. I've got a treat for you."

The smarmy whisper had no effect. She wasn't going to react to his faux kindnesses. She wouldn't speak to him again. She wouldn't even acknowledge his presence. She wasn't afraid of him anymore. After the first brutality and the horror of the last few days, what more could he do?

Yes, she ached all over and the collar around her neck was a nightmare of discomfort but, since the original attack, the man hadn't actually touched her in the ways that she had feared. She didn't understand it, but it gave her the strength to treat him with disdain.

Then she smelled the coffee. There was no mistaking the aroma.

"Come on, I brought you a nice breakfast."

Paper rustled and there was the scent of warm sugar. Her stomach rumbled. She rolled onto her back. As the chain clanked, the collar around her neck rubbed on the sore strip of skin and she hissed in pain.

He stood just inside the door with a cardboard cup and a bag in his hand. He held up the paper sack and waggled it in her direction.

"You want this, don't you? You have to want this. And look, a lovely warm drink."

The lights had flashed on so that the corridor behind him was dimmer and he was little more than a silhouette. He wasn't a big man, not young she didn't think, and at another time she was convinced she would have been able to fight him off, but not now, weak and weary.

Now the bravery ebbed away. *Why this? Why now?* Jean pushed herself upwards to sit with her back against the wall.

"Now then, no funny business, miss." He giggled. "Sit on your hands and close your eyes and you can have your treat."

She had no choice. How could she resist? Watching through slitted lids she saw him put the food onto a piece of cardboard and push it with a stick towards her. It was just like feeding a wild dog. Don't get too close. Don't take any risks.

"Okay. You can open your eyes. I'll be back later and maybe we'll have a chat."

The coffee was warm and sweet and strong. The croissant was fluffy and flaky. Jean thought she had never had anything so wonderful. Maybe with this inside her she would be stronger. Maybe the promised chat would give her hope. At least she may be able to find out why this had happened to her, and what he intended. She licked the crumbs from the paper bag and ran her finger around the bottom of the cup to get the last of the sugar and then she rested against the wall.

At first, she didn't notice the dizziness. She had felt so ill that weakness and bleariness had become normal. The room began to swim as her limbs became heavy. Her eyes wanted to close. All she wanted to do was sleep and she slipped away into the quiet.

The tiny camera in the corner of the room made a soft whirr as it tracked down. The lens zoomed in to take a closer look at her sagging mouth and her slumped shoulders and then the lights went out.

Chapter 31

"Shall we take my car?" Stella asked as they crossed the car park. Then she held up a finger as her phone rang.

"Yep, that's good," Jordan said.

As he waited for her to juggle with her bag and phone, Jordan looked up at the incident room window. There was a small group gathered looking down at them. He frowned.

"Are we wanted back in the office?"

"No, not as far as I know, why?"

"Nothing. It's okay. I just wondered if they were calling us back." He nodded at the phone in her hand.

"No, it's a mobile patrol patched through. They've found the *Jayne* out near Burscough. That's good, I didn't fancy driving all over the county looking for the damn thing. Did you need to go back?"

"No, sorry. It was just… oh look, it's fine. So, Burscough. Don't think I've been there."

"It's out in the sticks a bit. You know Ormskirk, don't you?"

"Yes, had a bit of a thing there a while back."

Stella pulled away from the Copy Lane station and headed for the A59.

"We've missed the rush hour, such as it is, so it'll probably take us about twenty minutes. When we get there can I ask you a favour?"

"Of course," Jordan said.

"Let me do the talking. This bloke really got on my tits the other day with his organ grinder comments."

"No problem, I'll stay schtum."

* * *

The little town wasn't busy. They crossed the canal on the road bridge and parked in the car park of the waterside restaurant.

A blue and white patrol car was tucked into the corner of the space alongside a retail and leisure area.

"We've kept out of the way, sir," said one of the officers in the car. "Don't think he knows he's been clocked."

"Okay, how far away is the barge?" Stella asked.

"About sixty metres or so, going left. There's a small line of boats, I think it was four, and he's on the very end. Do you want us to hang around?"

"If you would, that'd be great. We don't know how this is going to play out and it's possible we'll need prisoner transport. We'll see."

On the *Jayne* the curtains were drawn but the dog was outside in the transom. He was tethered with a piece of rope and had a blanket to lie on. As they approached, he raised his head and there was a short flap of his tail. Once they stopped he became more uneasy and dragged himself to his feet.

"Okay, boy. It's okay," Jordan said softly.

He held out a hand and the dog moved across the boards. He wasn't growling but he wasn't exactly making them welcome either.

"Mr Tranter. Can we have a word?" Stella called out. "Anybody home?"

There was no response.

"What do you reckon?" she said. "We've got a warrant, but that dog could be a problem."

"We'll just go in the other door, the one at the front," Jordan said. "He's safe here and that rope isn't long enough for him to jump off and come around."

"Yeah, of course."

As they turned to walk back along the bank, they spotted the figure of Billy Tranter heading towards them. He stopped and raised his chin, his hand sliding into the hip pocket of his baggy jeans.

Stella set off towards him.

"Careful, Stella," Jordan said.

"It's okay. I've got this." She pulled the warrant from her pocket and held it out in front of her.

"Need a word. Now, Billy."

The dog had seen its master and stood, front paws on the wooden rail surrounding the transom area. He was bouncing up and down on his back legs and barking intermittently.

As she passed Stella heard the slam of the door on the boat at the next mooring.

"Bloody hell, Tranter, shut that sodding dog up, will you?"

A fat man in a blue T-shirt and jogging bottoms pushed his way out of the cabin.

"Sod off, Jasper. Mind your own beeswax, yeah?"

"Okay, gents, let's just keep it down, shall we?" Jordan had left the excited dog and was a couple of paces behind Stella.

"Who the hell are you?" The man called Jasper was on the rear deck of his barge now. This one had no guard rails, and it would take a second for him to jump to the towpath.

Jordan held up his warrant card.

"DI Carr, sir. Would you just go back into your cabin? This doesn't need to concern you."

"Bloody druggy scum. You want to take him away. Him and that sodding mutt."

With that, Jasper turned and went back inside, where they could hear him talking loudly with a woman.

"Mr Tranter, I have a warrant here to search your boat," Stella shouted.

The boatman was obviously torn. He called to his dog.

"Scotty, it's all right, Scotty. Lay down, boy."

The dog quieted for a minute, but his eyes were still fixed on his owner. Jordan glanced back and for a minute was swept with sympathy for the confused animal.

"Come on, sir," he said. "Let's just get on with this. No point messing about."

He saw Stella's shoulders stiffen and knew that he had broken the agreement but he had seen no other option.

Tranter took another couple of steps towards them his hands now out by his side. Jordan began to relax, and Stella half turned to head back towards the *Jayne*. In that moment Tranter spun and jumped into a patch of shrubs and brambles on the embankment. Before either of them had a chance to react he had stormed through the undergrowth and out into the car park. Stella pulled out her airwaves set to raise the alarm as Jordan forced his way through the bushes and headed after the fleeing man. The dog was barking frantically, and Jasper reappeared brandishing a heavy piece of wood. The furore alerted the uniformed officers who were now haring along the towpath.

"Go back, he's in the car park." Stella waved her hands in the direction Tranter had fled.

They turned and sprinted back the way they had come.

She stood on the narrow strip of land, peered at the spiny bushes and the steep slope into the car park, glanced down at her lightweight jacket and shook her head.

"That went well," she muttered as she began to jog back to the parking area.

Jordan and the two uniformed men were making their way back to the retail section where a small crowd had gathered. Jordan shook his head.

"Gone. He knows his way around. He was away before I even got through the bushes. You guys, drive around. You know what he looks like. It's a rabbit warren of roads and streets around here. We'll take the other side of the bridge."

Stella shook her head. "I'm going back to the barge. I don't reckon he'll leave the dog. Not tied up outside."

"Okay. But keep in touch and I'll try and get some backup for a search of the area. Bloody hell, he can move."

Chapter 32

They hung about for a couple of hours. More cars came and Jordan showed the officers the mug shot image they had of Tranter.

"He's wearing baggy jeans and a denim jacket. He has shoulder-length dark hair, it's greasy. He's about five foot eight and skinny."

It was no good, he'd gone. Stella spent some of the time talking to Jasper and his wife. Their barge was neat and attractive with flowerpots on the roof alongside a few solar panels. It didn't help much. They didn't know Tranter and had only been involved with him because of the gangs of lads who had gathered beside his boat in the dark.

"I reckon he was selling them drugs," Jasper's wife said. "They were all drinking and messing about. Lots of barge owners like a drink and a barbie in the evening but it's always respectful and quiet. Not that horror. What are you going to do about the dog? I feel sorry for it. He's always yelling at it. I've never seen him hit it or anything and it's always got water and food. But you can't leave it there if he's buggered off. Dangerous, that is."

"Don't worry about the dog," Stella said. "I'll be leaving a uniformed officer here tonight and he'll make sure Scotty's okay. I don't suppose you've been down towards Old Roan in the last few weeks, have you?"

"No. We're heading that way, but we've only just set off. First trip of the season for us. Hope we don't have to put up with too many other people like that Tranter. It's not like it used to be." She shook her head and sighed.

"I reckon we might as well head back, Stella," Jordan said when she joined him back on the bank. "There're plenty of people looking for him."

"Yep. The DCI has been in touch. We're doing a television appeal about Jean Barker. He's doing the lead, but he wants me there. The press office has arranged for someone in Manchester to record a piece by Mel. I reckon Josh is getting a bit antsy because we're making so little progress."

"Trouble is that it's very possible the next development might well be the worst possible one."

It didn't need saying that he meant the gory discovery of remains in a wood or some deserted building.

"If she'd vanished from her walk, we could have suggested a reconstruction, but we just don't know what happened after that bloke saw her. All indications are that she went home safely and whatever happened was later," he continued.

"I know. There's nowhere to focus a search. We have an interview with the last yoga student – pupil – whatever you call them. He's coming into the station this affie. I'm not really hoping for much from him. Actually I reckon I'll let that lad Grice have a go at him. Be good practice and it's only a formality. We've already confirmed that he was where he was supposed to be so it's just a case of tidying that up a bit. We can double-check his timeline, but I already feel as though it's a waste of time."

Jordan nodded. "Listen, I've had a call from David Griffiths at St Anne Street. He wants a word, so I'll head down there first."

"He's not going to take you off this case, is he?"

"He hasn't said so. Mind you, up to now I don't know how much help I've been anyway, what with Nana Gloria and all of that."

"Well, just promise me you'll try to stick with me for a bit because I won't kid you, I'm floundering here."

"I'll do my best. See you later. Stay cool, things'll start to move soon."

As he spoke, he leaned to touch her shoulder and she nodded and smiled.

Chapter 33

It had only been a few days since Jordan had been in the office at St Anne Street, but already his desk was littered with empty cups, various papers and, oddly, a pair of nitrile gloves. He scooped the lot into a waste bin. It was unsettling. He had never fitted in. He had known it from the beginning and couldn't put his finger on why. David Griffiths had been glad to see him, and they had formed a friendship outside of work. It wasn't close, but enough to share a meal now and then, and have a chat on the phone about things other than police business.

Maybe it was the caseload that didn't suit him. They had worked together on several cases and most had come to a satisfactory conclusion. But for every gang or organisation they broke up and brought to some sort of justice, there were always more. Trafficking, drugs, arms, people. Money laundering, fraud. It was overwhelming at times. They were only ever catching the tail while the head of the serpent was still alive and probably always would be. Was that why? Was that why he had quite frankly found the work unfulfilling? Was that the reason? Or perhaps it was just the set-up. Many cases involved months and months of work which could fall apart in days.

The cops he was working with hadn't been unfriendly. Mostly they were Scousers and they didn't do unfriendly. Unless of course you were a Mancy or put on airs. Woollybacks were tolerated. After all someone had to live on the Wirral, didn't they? Even Mancs would have the support of their colleagues if in a bind, but it was best to keep out of the conversations about football and Manchester clubs. No, it wasn't unfriendliness exactly and certainly he had found less racism here than in many parts of his life. It was just that he had never formed the closeness that he had with Stella and before her with Terry Denn. Down on the streets with the ordinary people and the ordinary crimes. Yes, that was what he wanted. He would speak to David Griffiths and ask his advice but thinking now about Jean Barker and the woman from the canal, he knew for sure that he wanted to go back to what he did before.

"Jordan. We'll have a coffee in my office if that's okay."

Griffiths held out a hand in greeting and then drew it back.

"Oh, are we back to doing that now or still bumping elbows or the Prince of Wales bowing to each other thing?"

"Tell you what, let's just say hello," Jordan said.

"Fair enough."

One thing about the DCI's office was he always had decent coffee. Today there were even a couple of muffins on the table.

"Couple things I wanted to have a chat about," Griffiths said.

"Cool. Actually I wouldn't mind a natter with you sometime. Not now, later when we have time."

"Yeah. I think that's a good idea."

He knew, didn't he? He knew this wasn't working.

"First of all – this case you've got."

"Jean Barker?" Jordan asked.

"No, not that one. The other one. The body that they fished out of the Leeds and Liverpool Canal. I think I might have something that could be of interest. Something that might link back to us in Serious and Organised."

Chapter 34

They poured coffee and sat at the small table in the corner. Informal then, Jordan thought. He was relieved.

"I've been following what you were doing out there at Copy Lane," Griffiths said. "Not checking up as such, but I need to be able to explain, when I'm asked, about my team's deployment. I know you haven't made much progress with your missing woman. That has to be hard with her being a friend of your wife's. How is Penny by the way?"

"She's fine. Yeah, doing great now. Well, taking into account all the crap we've just been dealing with. She's working from home a lot; she likes it. The nursery had to close because of infections among the staff. Harry had to stay at home, so it was the only way. Getting back to normal now though."

"I heard you'd taken some personal time."

Jordan wondered who had been sharing information. He had only taken a few hours when he needed to call the family. There was no official record.

"Oh yes. Nana Gloria. She's not been well. In hospital."

"Oh, mate. That's crap. How is she?"

"It's hard not being able to see her, but I spoke to my mum this morning and she's doing better. They are sending her home with Mum to look after her. The other option was a care home and none of us would have gone along with that. As for the case, Jean Barker isn't really a friend of ours. Penny knows her daughter. There's no problem with me working on that."

"Okay. Good. You getting on okay with DS May?"

"Yep. We always did. She's great."

"Hmm, good. Well then, the other case. The young woman from the canal. I've seen the post-mortem examination report. It rang a little bell in here." He tapped his forehead. "A bit ago we had a grim situation. It was all mixed up with trafficking and porn sites. Some really nasty videos. Picked up by a charity who review abusive images and alert us to them. These originated in Eastern Europe as far as we can tell. They were already on to it over there and there is still an investigation ongoing. Being totally frank we're sidelined at the moment. We're still working with European forces where we can, but there's no doubt there has been a change since we split from Europol. It's subtle but it's there. Anyway, I had our people dig out the footage. I've got it set up to go on my machine. I think it's best if you just have a look at it and then we'll see what you think. It's not nice."

On the screen the space looked like a cellar or basement of some sort. The walls were dark stone and damp-looking. The lighting was dim at first but slowly the illumination increased until the scene directly in front of the camera was revealed.

It seemed deliberate, like the opening of a film. It was taken from a high level looking down onto what at first appeared to be a bundle of rags. There was the rattle of a lock, and a narrow beam of light lit the scene quite suddenly. The bundle moved, groaned, and shuffled back towards the wall. A figure dressed in dark clothes and with a loose hood pulled low over the head appeared carrying a long stick and what seemed to be a small square box. The person bent and pushed the box across the flagstones with the pole.

As they retreated to stand before the half-open door, the creature who was crouched against the wall reached to take hold of the box and pull it closer. They dragged out the contents. The woman drank greedily. For it was clear now that the decrepit heap on the floor was a woman. Thin and dirty. She was gulping the drink, wiping at her face with the back of her hand. She reached again and brought out a handful of food which she stuffed into her mouth. She drank again, ate again and then snatched up the box and lowered her head into it to lick at the bottom and the sides.

The figure by the door hammered with the end of the stick and she pushed the box away and scuttled back to the corner.

"That's a bloke, isn't it?" Jordan said.

"Almost certainly. You'll see in a minute a glimpse of his shoes."

The stick was brought down again with several sharp taps.

She fell forward now onto her hands and knees and crawled across the floor until she was kneeling in front of the man. He held out his foot towards her. She bent close and kissed the toes.

"Jesus. That's enough," Jordan said. "What the hell was that?"

"That's not the worst one. We have seen some where the women were beaten and one where the poor thing was obviously dead."

"Where are they?"

"Still don't know for sure. As with all this stuff, the origin of the video is so cleverly hidden that it's almost impossible to trace it. There is a pretty big team working on it, I believe, and we have been helping as much as we can under present circumstances. There's no speech. All communication is with that bloody staff. It indicates a degree of brainwashing or training, so we don't know how long these poor sods have been kept. The trouble is that in some of these countries, girls set off for the lights of the city. It's the same old story. They are full of high hopes but when things go wrong, they get involved in the darker side of life. They don't want to go home with their tails between their legs and the families are afraid or ashamed or even, in some cases, disinterested. They don't report them missing. The main thing I wanted you to notice, though, was this."

Griffiths zoomed into a close view of the woman as she crawled across the flagstones.

"Yes. I see it. A collar around her neck, and the leash. Is that leather?"

"As far as we can tell, yes."

"So do we think this is happening here? In the UK, I mean."

"With the discovery of your woman in the water it very much seems like a possibility. So, we want this now to come under the auspices of Serious and Organised and as you're already on site and up to speed it couldn't be better."

"What, you want to take it away from DS May?" Jordan said.

"If you think she can help, keep her on board, but you'll be SIO from now on and it'll be on the books here."

"That's hardly fair, Dave."

"She hasn't got very far with it anyway."

"No, but it's early days and it'll look bad for her."

"I'm sure you can put it over so she sees the sense in it. From what I hear you and her are pretty close these days."

"What's that supposed to mean?"

"Oh, nothing, just that you seem like a tight team. Come on, let's get a pint while the boffins put all this stuff together for you. It's not pleasant viewing but you can share it with your mate out at Copy Lane."

"Actually, Dave, I reckon I'd best get home. Can you arrange to have that stuff sent to me?"

"As you like. However, a word to the wise, Jordan. You know what it's like, there's a lot of gossiping in the force and some of it is just out to cause trouble. Watch how you go."

Chapter 35

Penny was in the kitchen when Jordan arrived at home in Crosby. The baby was playing with a couple of carrot sticks on the table of his highchair. The house was warm and there was the scent of garlic and tomatoes. It was just what Jordan needed. On the way back from the city centre he had almost called Stella a couple of times. Then he had seen the sense in waiting until he had a chance to absorb all that had just happened.

Who was it in Aintree who had been reporting back to David Griffiths? It might be fairly innocent. It could just be colleagues talking, very probably DCI Martin. But there was a bigger problem. How the hell was he supposed to tell Stella that he was taking over the case of the woman in the canal? She was his friend. She was trying to make her way and it was early days for her at the station in Copy Lane. To have this case, a major investigation, whipped out from under her was bad enough, but to have it given to him, whom she thought of as a friend, was beyond awkward.

"Are you alright, love? You look done in." Penny poured a glass of red wine and pulled a chair out from under the kitchen table. "Here, take the weight off. I've defrosted one of your lasagnas and I thought we might wait until Harry was in bed and maybe have a quiet romantic meal, candles and stuff, in the dining room. We haven't been out for ages, but we could make this do.

Anyway your lasagna stands up against anything we can get around here."

He took the glass and finished half the wine in one long drink. "I needed that."

"Problems?" She walked over, wrapped her arms around his shoulders and nuzzled his neck.

"Just work stuff. Nothing for you to bother about. I like the idea of a date night. Let's do that. I'll take Harry and give him his bath. I must make one call and then I'm all yours. Penny…"

"What?" She was at the other side of the room chopping salad.

"You do know, don't you, that you are my life? You know that nothing, absolutely nothing, is more important than you. You know, don't you? You are the only thing that matters. Well you and Harry."

She turned to him, frowning. "Hey, what's all this? Of course I know that. Are you okay?"

He shook his head and took another drink. "Yes, sorry. I'm fine. It's just been an odd day. Take no notice. I'll see to the baby and maybe we should open that good bottle of red we've been saving."

"Nice. I'll open it. Let it breathe."

She watched him leave the kitchen with their son in his arms and turned back to the salad prep. The pandemic had taken its toll on everyone, but her husband was a rock. He stood firm against everything. She was shaken by the look on his face, the sag of his shoulders. She heard him chatting to Harry as he ran the bath. He sounded fine now, laughing with their son, but she was thrown. She knew he was worried about Nana, but what had prompted that outburst?

Chapter 36

"Jordan, what can I do for you?" Stella answered on the second ring.

"I need a word. Can you talk right now?"

"I can. Just waiting for my pizza delivery. How did things go at St Anne Street? You didn't let him take you back there, did you?"

"No. That didn't happen."

Suddenly it felt wrong to be telling her this way. He needed to talk face to face and let her know that as far as he was concerned, she was still vital to the inquiry, and he would work with her. Maybe there would be a way to fix this, so the rest of the team didn't need to know. He needed time. Luck was on his side as he heard the chime over the phone.

"Is that your bell?"

"Yeah, hang on, let me go and get the door."

"No, listen, it wasn't urgent. No need to interrupt your dinner. I'll speak to you in the morning."

"Are you sure? I'll only be a mo."

"Really. Take a break. See you tomorrow. Maybe in early?"

"Yep. Sevenish?"

"Great."

It was almost ten when she rang him back. Jordan was in the living room with Penny. There was jazz on the sound system and rum in the glasses. He'd put away the worry for the moment. Nana Gloria always said 'sufficient unto the day is the evil thereof.' He wasn't sure what it meant exactly and thought it might be something from the Bible, but it seemed to suit the purpose. He would tackle the problems tomorrow. But now, the phone rang and as he moved his wife's drowsy head from where it rested on his shoulder, he knew that he was going out. It was a second sight of a sort. Some calls just held the threat of work and that was it.

"Stella, everything okay?"

"Yes. Sorry, Jordan. Penny'll hate me."

Penny heard and shouted across the settee, "No I don't, it's the bad guys I hate."

"Well they've picked up Tranter. He was spotted on the canal bank in Burscough. Worried about his dog. It's just as well as the bloody thing was becoming a bit of an issue. We couldn't keep a plod on the canal bank forever. We should really have had it taken to the pound. Anyway, I've got them bringing it to the station. I know I should have called the dog warden and had it taken to the kennels, but I told the uniform blokes to tell him he should come and pick it up from Copy Lane. I thought it might make him a bit more amenable rather than just hauling him in. Although I'll admit part of me just didn't want to think of it shut in a cage wondering what was happening. It hasn't done anything wrong after all."

"Are you going to question him now?" he asked.

"I thought it'd be best, otherwise we are just wasting time and he'll walk. You can be sure he knows his rights and we haven't got anything we can charge him with yet. Betting is he'll grab the pooch and be away."

"I'll meet you there."

Chapter 37

As Jean fought her way back to consciousness the overriding emotion was despair. But there was no help for it. She was still alive. She was cold, colder than she had been before. As her senses recovered, she understood that she was in a different place. The walls were darker, but there was more leakage of light through a window high up in the wall. A small slit of a thing. Although the glass was not clear there was nothing covering it. She could see the light from an almost full moon and now and then the shadow of a cloud.

She pushed herself up into a sitting position and stretched, tilting her chin upwards, tipping her head as far back as she could manage, peering towards the grey oblong. She felt a frisson of excitement. She took a deep breath. There was something else different and for a while she struggled to work out what it was.

It was the smell. She recognised the acrid aroma of damp and a vague stench of animals. She could detect standing water, stagnant and unpleasant. There had been none of that in the other place, just dust and the faint odour of humans.

What did this change mean? Okay, she had been drugged and while she was out for the count, she had been moved. Was that good? Probably not. She had given up hoping for good. But still, there was something here to think about, something to concentrate on.

Animals. Maybe a farm, not a zoo surely. The safari park at Knowsley? No, she was being silly, that was impossible, she would be able to hear people, wouldn't she? Had they reopened? She didn't know and anyway it was night-time. If it was a farm, there had to be people. Animals needed to be cared for regularly. She tried to call out. Her throat was sore and all she managed was a rough croak. She tried again, gathering saliva in her mouth and coughing, but it was no use. No-one would ever hear the feeble sound.

She rattled the chain around her neck. The ring that fastened it to the wall clattered and knocked, but it was still not enough to be heard outside this space. She took in a deep breath, screwed her eyes tight, threw back her head and howled. No words, no attempt at making sense. Just a howl with every atom of fear and desperation feeding into it. She screamed until her eyes ran with tears and her raw throat forced her to stop.

As she opened her eyes again, bright lights blinded her. She screwed her lids closed and turned away. As she dared to open them again her eyes picked up a small red glow in the corner of the room.

As her eyes became more accustomed to the light and her head began to clear, she could make out the shape of the camera. As she watched, the lens adjusted, it was zooming in. Of all the things that had happened to her, of all the horrors that the recent days had brought, this was the worst. She was being observed. In her filth and her misery she was being watched, and now she understood about the lights. She looked around the room. The bucket stood in the corner within the reach of the chain. It had been in the other place, or one like it. She gasped aloud. Had she been watched there? Had someone seen her shame and her disgrace? She couldn't remember and didn't try too hard because the thought of it was sickening.

She hadn't believed that she could feel any worse but now the idea that she was being seen by someone unknown and remote was horrific. She closed her eyes and rocked back and forth, accompanied by the rattle of the swinging chain, and she groaned as the lights went out.

In the other place she had heard him coming, heard the slap of his shoes on a hard floor, but here the first she knew was when the door creaked open and a dark figure appeared in the space, backlit by the moonlight.

Chapter 38

"Are you okay to drive?" Penny asked.

"No, I'm getting an Uber."

"But why not get a patrol car to pick you up?"

"I don't think it'd be any quicker. They have enough to deal with and they're short on bods everywhere. It's sod's law that while they're ferrying me there'll be some sort of a flap and they won't be available. No. I've booked a taxi. He'll be here in a couple of minutes. Sorry, love. It was a really nice evening."

"Yeah. Well, we had that, and I have always known this is what you get when you marry a copper."

Jordan leaned and buried his face in the cloud of her dark hair. She smelled a little of the cooking, but he didn't mind that.

"I love you, Pens."

"I know. Now, go and sort out this dog and his master."

"Ha. Yes. It's a nice dog. Maybe when Harry's older we could–"

"Don't go there, Mr Carr. While we are both at work we are not getting a dog. When you retire I might let you have a big dog so you can keep fit taking it for walks. Go on, I heard your cab. Take care, Jordan."

"Always."

* * *

Billy Tranter was already irate and swearing when they walked into the interview room. In an attempt to keep him under control Stella had asked that they put him in one of the softer rooms. Here there were chairs grouped around a table, but they were more comfortable than the upright metal ones screwed to the floor in the other spaces. There were still panic alarms around the walls and the recording equipment was the same.

"Where's my dog? What have you done with him?"

"He's okay, Mr Tranter. They've given him a drink and some biscuits," Stella said. "I've just seen him and he's fine."

"Good. He'd better be. Now, give him back and let me get off."

"We'd like to have a bit of a chat, if you don't mind," Jordan said.

"Well, I do mind. I've done nothing and I've seen nothing. I've already told every bloody rozzer that asked. Now, if you don't mind." He stood and walked to the door.

"We really could do with your help, Billy."

"Aye, well, I can't help you. Unless you're going to arrest me for some bloody trumped-up charge, I'm off."

"Your neighbour in the other barge tells us you've been dealing drugs to youths on the canal bank," Stella said.

"Well, I never, so you can tell him to mind his own sodding business. Nosey old fart."

"I did see you myself, Billy. We both know that wasn't Old Holborn ready rubbed you were stuffing in your pipe," Stella said.

"I've got arthritis, it helps with the pain. A bit of weed and there's all this? No bloody wonder you lot are short of money."

"We wanted to ask you about the body that we found floating in the canal not far from where your boat was moored," Jordan said. "Poor woman had been treated badly and that's a terrible way for someone to end up. You must see that."

"Nothing to do with me."

"You saw nothing at all? She must have made a noise when she went in. We reckon she went off the bridge. That'd make a bit of a splash that would," Stella said.

He paused at the door, his hand on the knob. He turned back. "It was nothing to do with me. Nothing, you understand."

"What was nothing to do with you?" Jordan asked. They were breaking through. "Have you had anything to eat, Billy? We could send out to Maccie Ds for you. A burger, some chips."

"Think you can bribe me with bloody fast food crap?"

"No, not at all. I just thought, as you're here, and it's late, you might have trouble getting something. Not many places open at the moment, are there?"

"Tell you what. You get me a bacon butty and I'll stay till it's eaten. Proper bacon in a barm cake with butter."

"We can get you one of those from the canteen. Coffee, tea, Coke?"

"Don't suppose you could run to a beer."

"Sorry, no, not allowed."

"Look, I'll tell you what I know and it's not much. Then you let me have my dog, let me go and sodding well leave me be. I've not done nothing. Okay I might have given a few lads a treat but that's just what I'm like. That's what I am. Kind. Known for it."

"Okay, let me just get on it. You'll be okay here for a minute, yeah?" Jordan said.

Back in the corridor he frowned down at Stella.

"What are the chances? This time of night, bacon? We've nothing to hold him on so it's the only thing we can do. Probably shouldn't have promised that."

"Leave it with me, mate. I'll have a word with Marjorie. She's a gem, is Marjorie, and a bingo mate of my mam's. Night cover in the canteen and worth her weight in gold."

Stella laughed. "With Marj that's a lot of gold. Go and make a brew, I'll be back in a bit."

Chapter 39

The smell of bacon in the confined interview room was torment. Jordan could feel his belly rumbling as they waited for Billy Tranter to plough his way through the two rolls, butter dripping onto the paper plate, ketchup smearing his mouth. He strung it out, slurped at the mug of builder's tea, and picked at his teeth with his thumbnail.

"Billy, when you're ready," Stella said.

"Yeah. Well. Like I said, I don't know nothing." He grinned at them. He knew they'd be wondering if they'd wasted time, energy and food just to get themselves nowhere. After a pause he nodded.

"Right," he said. "I'm never going to say this in no court or nothing like that so don't even bother asking. I'm telling you once, now, and then that's it done."

Jordan glanced at the recording equipment. It was possible Tranter had forgotten that he had restarted it when they came back into the room. Or maybe he was fully aware and somewhere inside he really did want to help.

They didn't dare to hope that it might be the breakthrough they needed, but maybe. They sat in silence and waited as he pushed the chair back from the table and stretched out his legs in front of him.

"So I was moored in the usual place I go to when I visit Old Roan. I've got a couple of customers there. And before you start putting two and two together and coming up with seven, they're people I do gardens for. Every few weeks I mow their grass and occasionally cut their bushes.

You can ask them if you like. I'll give you their names. I'm not what you think. You see me and you see where I live and you think I'm a no-mark; you think I'm some sort of dropped-out druggie."

"We haven't made any sort of judgement," Jordan said.

"Like hell you haven't. I'm not a divvy. I just choose how I live. Anyway, I'm not talking about me. Like I said, I was moored up there. I hadn't been for a while because of all this social distancing and what have you, but stuff seems to be getting better so I thought I'd give it a go. Well, the woman I was supposed to be working for said she didn't want me coming round in case I had a virus. Silly bitch. Where did she think I was going to get a virus? Out the canal? As it happened it was raining so I told her I'd come back in a few days. I told her I'd do a test. Silly mare went along with that. Anyway I had a bifter, just an ordinary ciggy, nothing dodgy, and a couple of jars and settled down with my book. Yeah, I can read an' all."

Neither detective spoke. He had a chip on his shoulder, but maybe he had reason, and now he was speaking they wouldn't risk annoying him.

"Anyway, late, probably about two in the morning, I heard this shouting. A right barny. More than one bloke, I reckon. I had a quick scan and they were on the bank. I've had trouble before with people nicking stuff, so I got up and went out. Took me cosh with me but left the dog inside. He's a good lad and knows when not to make any fuss. There were two blokes. By the time I got out they were past me and running up the steps onto the bridge. I couldn't see up on to the road from where I was but the next thing there's this splash and something was in the water."

"What did you do?" Jordan asked.

"I minded my own business, that's what I did. I went back into my cabin and had my smoke."

"You didn't go out to see what had fallen in?"

"Nope. Not with blokes on the bridge and all the shouting that had gone on. Look" – he sat straight in the chair – "I'm knocking on a bit now. I'm doing okay but I'm not as young as I was and I'm not up to thumping big blokes and I'm certainly not up to being thumped. The best thing to do in situations like that is keep your beak out. I kept my beak out, and next morning I went back up to Burscough. I gave it a day and I reckoned that whatever had gone on would be all taken care of. I wouldn't have come back at all for a bit, but I was boracic, I needed the job, so I came back. You lot were there, and I answered the questions and that was that."

"You told us at first you hadn't seen anything," Stella said.

"Nor did I. I heard some shouting. I heard a splash. You often hear splashes. Have you any idea of the stuff people throw in the canal? Bikes, prams, blocks of bloody concrete."

"Yes, we've seen."

"Well there we are then. Nothing to do with me. Right. Get me my dog. I'm off. Thanks for the scran. Don't bother me again. I'm off anyway, this place has got too busy for me."

There was nothing they could do without evidence that he'd done anything wrong, and nothing was found in the search of his narrowboat. As Billy Tranter left the room Stella lowered her head to her folded hands on the tabletop and let out a sigh.

"Bugger, bugger, bugger. He doesn't know anything, does he?"

"No, I don't reckon he does," Jordan said.

"All a waste of time and manpower."

"Not entirely. He did tell us something we didn't know," Jordan said.

"What?"

"That there were very possibly men there and more than one."

"Tremendous, that's a great help. Okay, that's it, I'm off home. I'll see you in the morning."

Stella didn't wait for a reply but stomped down the corridor her shoulders slumped and her jacket trailing from her hand and along the tiles. Jordan hadn't the heart to speak to her now about the ongoing plan. Then again perhaps she would be glad to get rid of the case after all. Of course the other side of that was that he was going to be the one left floundering with hardly anything to go on and this hadn't been the plan when he'd gone to Jean Barker's house. He would need to speak to Mel in the morning and he had nothing to tell her.

Chapter 40

Jordan bought a breakfast of coffee and sugary buns from Starbucks. He felt bad about it, seeing them as a feeble sort of peace offering, but there hadn't been a war – not yet. He left them in the car. Then he felt bad about the waste and retrieved them.

"Scrummy." Stella tore open the bags. "Listen, last night I was a bit bummed, but you were right, you know. He did give us more information than we had before, and it could be important. So it's onward and upward. I'm going to get some of the team on the CCTV looking for two blokes, either on foot or in a car, and then out onto the bank. You never know, we could be lucky, and the roads would have been quiet because it was raining and very late."

She was reinvigorated, excited. As he geared up to speak the door opened and John Grice clomped into the room.

"John, good to see someone's keen. I've got a job for you," Stella said. "We need to find two blokes. Don't have any information except that they were together, on foot, on the bank. We don't know about before that – could have had a car. Probably had a car, actually. There is the vague chance that the woman was with them. Or she could have been running from them. Now, if you find that I'll have your babies." She stopped, and there was silence for a few seconds.

"Great, I'll let my boyfriend know," Grice said.

It could have been true that he was gay, but the main thing was that it snubbed out the embarrassment. Jordan glanced at Stella. She was beet red.

"Right, well, as I was saying, they may well appear to be agitated. Start at the Melling Road bridge and widen the scope. There are cameras at the retail park, some at the golf centre, the racing circuit. At that time of the night there should be hardly anyone about. Get on to it and when the civvies come in get a couple of them to give you a hand. I know there's very little there to work with, but you just never know." She paused and picked up her tablet. "Jordan. You and me are going to go back over all the stuff that we know about Jean Barker. We're missing something there. Err, that's if it's okay with you."

How could he burst her bubble?

"Yeah, good idea. One of us needs to speak to Mel later. There is one other thing. Just before we do I need to get you up to speed on some stuff to do with the canal woman."

"Oh right. What's that?"

"Yesterday, when I went down to St Anne Street, one of the reasons Griffiths called me in was because they'd had something come to light that might help us with the investigation."

For a minute she paused. He saw her process the information and come down on the side of hope.

"You'd better fill me in then."

He had a copy of the reports and images that he'd seen yesterday.

"This must mean that our woman is part of something bigger," Stella said.

"Yep. It could be that. Or maybe... well, I thought about it last night."

He didn't need to tell her that he'd sat all night in the dark living room struggling with his thoughts; trying to find a way out of the tangle.

"So the thinking is that this is out there on the internet, on the dark web. But I wondered if ours is possibly some sort of copycat. Someone has seen this video of the poor woman and thought, that's something I want to do."

"Jesus. Do you really think so?"

"I'm afraid I do. People copy everything they see, don't they? I mean why would you eat laundry liquid, for example, and yet a couple of years ago tons of kids were doing it. It's a sick world and there is no accounting for the evil that people will do, especially if they can make some money at it."

"So, are we supposed to work with Europol now then, or what?"

She was processing the developments. He could tell her now, but she was so upbeat he didn't.

"According to Griffiths the connection between the UK and Europe is inconclusive and they are struggling with it over there. It's a bigger investigation but they are far from solving it, from what I was told. There is no doubt that the woman from the canal had been treated in a similar way to the one in the video. The collar, the starvation and all of that. So, let's just carry on with our investigation. My thinking is that we should be looking for where she was kept. Deserted premises. Perhaps warehouses, that sort of thing. Let's just keep it simple for now. If we do find stuff that needs to be fed back, if you like, I'll handle that. You know, keep Serious and Organised up to speed. Now, how did she end up in the water? Did she escape? We know that she wasn't thrown into the water when she was dead, so, was she on the run? Trying to run from those blokes that Tranter heard? Was the water her only hope at that point? Desperate to get away she went into the canal, and she was so weak that she couldn't survive? Was she knocked unconscious, and they left her and ran?"

"Bloody Nora. It doesn't bear thinking about, does it? You didn't say anything last night about the other woman. Why was that?"

"Sorry, I should have done but I needed to get my head around it."

"And David Griffiths, what are his thoughts?"

"Oh well, he just wants us to get on with it and try to make progress."

She didn't speak but the look she gave him was what Nana Gloria would have described as 'old-fashioned'. Jordan opened up another file on his computer and scrolled down.

"As for Jean Barker, the only thing I can think of right now is to go back to her house. We know she was seen by the canal so we could do that walk. There aren't many routes to get from her home to where she was seen. I can't imagine right now what it might show us but unless the bloke that rang us gets back in touch, we still have absolutely nothing except that it's the last sighting."

"Nothing until her body turns up. Sorry but I don't see how it's going to end any other way. Not unless we are granted a miracle and they seem to be in short supply. Oh, how is your Nana?"

"Home today. Bed rest but, thank heavens, I think she's come through it and she's testing negative for the virus. If that's our full allowance of miracles then I'll take it, thank you."

Chapter 41

"Okay, Jean's house. I'll drive if you like," Stella said. "What happened to the cat?"

"Mel took him back with her to Manchester. We would have looked after him, but Penny has an allergy to cat hair, so it wasn't really a good idea."

"Nothing came back from the cast they made of the shoe print here. It was a trainer type. Very common and available absolutely everywhere. Slightly worn but that only helps if we find it. No real sign of a limp or anything. Let's face it, the prints could have been made by the dustbin man or a window cleaner."

"Good point. I wonder if she had tradespeople going round. Have we asked?"

"We have. No-one. And Mel says she does her own garden," Stella said.

"So, not Tranter. That would have been too good to be true."

"No, not him, I'm afraid. Jean seems to have been almost a recluse."

Stella's phone rang. "It's Grice. Shit, I can't believe I made that stupid comment this morning. What am I like?"

"Don't worry about it. It's just something people say."

"Yes, but I shouldn't have. I have to up my game, don't I? I know I sometimes speak before my brain's engaged. I need to be more careful."

Was she fishing? Jordan gave something between a shake and a nod of the head. He could say something now, but the moment had passed, and he had made a decision. If David Griffiths was angry then so be it. He was kidding himself. Griffiths would definitely be angry, and he could be in deep trouble. He'd ignored a direct order. If they solved the case, he might get away with this, but he knew he was digging himself a deep hole.

"Right," Stella said, "he says he's found something."

"Okay, let's leave Jean's place till later. Actually, that fits in well, I was thinking there might be some mileage in talking to the yoga class again; they have a meeting today in the hall if things are still on schedule."

* * *

At his desk in the incident room John Grice was surrounded. The others moved aside to make room for Jordan and Stella.

"That was quick work, John," Jordan said.

"It was pure luck, boss. These things often are, aren't they? Anyway I'll just let you have a look, that's best."

On the screen they watched the dark image of a van pulling off the Ormskirk Road and onto the Racecourse Business Park. Everywhere was deserted as they sped through the empty parking lot. The vehicle skidded at speed around the corner of the DIY warehouse and along a narrow access road.

"We lose them then. You can see they leave the car. But it's not a good image of them. Too far away and a bad angle. But they were on their toes pretty sharpish. I've already sent a copy to the forensic imaging department. They'll do what they can to improve it. Anyway, they were gone for about an hour. The time is right given what you told me, and from there they can access the canal bank. There is a fence, but if someone wanted to get over it badly enough there are ways, especially with two of them. They could bunk up or climb on something. Then they're onto the racetrack and, quick as you like, the canal bank. I've put in a call to the racecourse owners to see if they have coverage. I don't expect they would have on this area of the grounds. Round the buildings there is CCTV but that's a fair distance away and there was no meeting on at the time, shame really. The golf centre is covered but again it's just the buildings. Nothing over by the canal to nick or damage really, except a couple of thousand balls I suppose."

"That's absolutely brilliant, John. Really great," Stella said. "Have you been able to get a plate number?"

"Not yet but there's a couple of us working on it and the guys in forensic imaging are on to that as well. Given time we can track this van back, and hopefully find where it came from. It'll just take a while because he wasn't on the main roads all the time. I reckon he came from Switch Island. That means that he could have come in from any direction before that, so it's going to be a lot of viewing. We're on it though."

"That's excellent. Leave that with some of the others and you and one of the uniforms get down there and have a look on the ground. Where they parked, where you can see them running. If you think there's any point, we'll get a scene of crime team down. Trouble is it's been a while. Anyway, keep me updated," Stella said. "Me and Jordan are off out again. Going to Old Roan to the yoga place. If you have anything, get me on my mobile."

Stella turned and threw her keys to Jordan.

"You drive, will you? I want to study this area on my tablet."

"Ooh," one of the civilians said. "Driving the new car, you must be in favour, sir."

There was a ripple of laughter as they walked from the room.

"Pillocks," Stella muttered. "Sorry but sometimes I find all the joking a bit much. We have one dead woman and one missing and they're larking about."

"It's the way people handle things sometimes, isn't it? You know that," Jordan said.

"Yes, I know. It's just…"

"What?"

"Okay," she said, "if you must know, somebody told me that there's been talk."

"Talk?"

"Yes. Don't know which stupid prat started it but if I find out I'll swing for them. Gossiping and tattling. *'Oh yes, The DS and the DI, they're always out together. Oh, they've gone to get their breakfast.'* And then stuff about us going in the same car. Stupid buggers, of course we do.

"Ah."

"Ah?"

"Yes. Ah. When I was with Dave Griffiths, he made a couple of comments that I couldn't quite get my head around. Now they make more sense. Asking about me and Penny, asking about how I was getting on with you. For heaven's sake, this is ridiculous."

"Is that why you've been a bit odd since that meeting?"

"Odd? I haven't been odd," Jordan said.

"Yes, you have. A bit… withdrawn."

"No, no I haven't. I didn't know, did I? Not till just now."

"Is there something else then?" she asked.

He was saved by the bell on his phone. "Sorry, it's Karen."

Stella simply nodded. He couldn't ignore the DCI's secretary.

"Sorry, Kas, I'm out at the moment." Jordan raised his eyebrows in warning and Stella made a zipping movement across her lips. "Maybe later? … Oh right, okay. Well, I'll wait to hear."

As he slid the phone back into his pocket Stella turned away and headed towards the door.

"The DCI wants a word. I'm not in the right mood just now. Anyway after this morning he's unavailable for the next couple of days. Tied up in meetings apparently, out of town."

"Hmm. I wonder what he's after?"

"Guess we'll find out soon enough," Jordan said.

He could guess what this was. Griffiths had been in touch about the new arrangements. Right now, his mind was like minestrone soup and he needed to get his head straight. Later he'd have to sit down with Stella and come clean.

Chapter 42

There was dust in the corners of the corridor and the air in the community centre felt stagnant.

"Doesn't look as though it's open. Maybe they've put it off?" Stella said.

"There were a few cars in the car park so there's somebody here."

They walked through the empty rooms.

"It's good things are opening up again," Jordan said. "It makes you think it'll all be okay in the end."

"Do you really think so? Sometimes it seems that the old life has gone, and we are going to live like this forever. I mean, I know we're not locked down or anything, but I still think there's a funny feeling around some times."

"Keep the faith, it's all you can do. Here we go – up there, look, the door's open and the lights are on."

The aroma here was different, they recognised the incense from Veronica Surr's house. In the assembly hall yoga mats were spread wide apart and all the windows were open, but a small group were kneeling with one leg stuck out behind them. Veronica Surr was at the front of the room murmuring encouragement. She turned as Stella pushed open the door and held up her hand in a 'wait a minute' gesture.

They stepped back into the corridor and leaned against the wall. A figure crossed the passageway carrying a mop and dragging a bucket on wheels. He glanced at them and stopped. As he walked towards them, Jordan went to meet him.

"Afternoon, sir." He held up his warrant card. "We're just waiting for the yoga teacher."

"Oh aye, what's she been up to then?"

"Nothing. We just want to have a word with her about an ongoing inquiry."

"All in there, are they? Twisting and writhing in their underwear."

"That's not quite what I saw," Jordan answered, "but yes there is a class going on. Are you the caretaker?"

"Well I'm not trailing this about for the good of my health." He jangled the handle of the bucket as he spoke.

Jordan showed him the printed image of Jean Barker. "Do you know this woman?"

"Dunno. Might do. Might be one of them." He pointed to the yoga classroom.

"Have you seen her lately?" Stella flashed her ID as she spoke.

"No, just back today that lot. Classes are drifting back in dribs and drabs. I liked it better before, just me and the mice." The caretaker gave a short cackle.

"So, when was the last time you saw this lady?"

"Can't say for sure. Probably before all that palaver." He pointed at a coloured notice referencing social distancing and mask-wearing. Then he nodded towards the opening door at the end of the corridor.

"There you go. Mrs Stretch and Bend's out now."

"Thank you, Mr…"

"Brian. Brian Beetham, that's me. Not that it's any of your business anyway." With that he slouched away, the long mop rattling against the bucket.

"Nice bloke," Stella said.

"Ha. Not exactly sweetness and light, was he?"

Veronica Surr stood by the door which she closed softly. "They're in Shavasana. Won't be very long. Can I help you?"

"We just thought we'd pop in and have another word if that's okay," Stella said. "Just in case anyone has any more thoughts about Mrs Barker. When they're out of Shavawhatever of course."

"You still haven't found her?"

"I'm afraid not."

"You won't now, will you? That poor woman. I wonder what on earth can have happened to her."

As she spoke Surr's eyes filled with tears which gathered on her lids and flowed unhindered down her face to drip onto the blue stretchy top she wore.

"We haven't given up," Jordan said. "We won't give up, not until we have solved this."

"Yes, well. We'll see, won't we?" With the cryptic comment Surr turned and walked back into the room.

Chapter 43

The smell woke Jean. Tomatoes, onions, garlic. She didn't want to open her eyes because surely once she did it would be gone. This was some sort of delirium, it had to be. In spite of dehydration her mouth watered, and her stomach growled. She was as awake now as she could manage these days and still it was there. She sniffed.

"Come on now. Open your eyes."

The man was in the doorway. Daylight behind him. Impossible to say what time. The light was grey and overcast.

"Can you smell that? Can you? Mmmm. Lovely, isn't it? I bet you like that. Spaghetti, pasta, and lovely sauce.

Hmmm. And a drink. I would have brought you wine, but I don't think you're well enough. Maybe later we can do that. But now there's lovely fizzy water. Look, I even put some ice cubes in it." He rattled the plastic beaker. "Come on now, don't let the food go cold."

Jean had shuffled herself upright with her back against the wall. She swallowed.

"Please," she said.

"Oh yes. It's for you. Of course it is. You just have to be nice first."

Her heart clenched. Was this it? Was this when he raped her? She shuffled back and drew up her knees.

"Oh come on now, don't be getting upset. All you need to do is let me see just how much you want this and how grateful you are."

She couldn't speak, tears flooded her eyes. She could barely breathe. She glanced around in panic but there was nothing she could do. Surely, he wouldn't touch her, not filthy as she was, tethered to the wall and stinking. She couldn't bear the smell of herself; how could he even think of it?

"Now, what you have to do is just come over here. You have to come here, and you have to offer up your thanks. Just like the slave girls used to do. It's not a lot to ask and then you can have this lovely dinner."

"I don't know what you mean," she whispered.

"It's easy. I am near enough so just crawl over here and lick my boots and then you can have your food."

"What? No, you can't make me do that."

"Yes, yes, I can. Well, it's up to you really. Maybe you need more training, but you could make this quick and easy. Just crawl over here, lick my boots and then you can eat."

Jean glanced into the corner of the room. The little light on the camera burned red and she began to understand.

"You sick bugger. You filthy sick excuse for a human. How can you? How can you do this? You vile creature."

He shook his head and bent to leave the plate against the wall, out of her reach.

"I'll leave this here as a reminder of how this could have been, what you could have had."

The door slammed as he left. The lights stayed on for a while and she didn't move. She wouldn't give him the satisfaction.

Eventually she curled back into a ball and tucked herself into the corner.

Chapter 44

"What exactly are you hoping to gain?" Veronica Surr asked. "You've questioned us already and nobody knows anything. We haven't even seen each other in the flesh until today, not for weeks."

"Sometimes when you think about things for a few days something will come to mind," Stella said. "Did Jean Barker ever talk about going away? Maybe she said something just in passing over coffee and drinks or later in the Zooms. You know the sort of thing – what she wanted to do once we were out of lockdown. Did she ever talk about meeting people, perhaps confide about a new relationship?"

As she spoke Stella had turned to the group and watched as they shook their heads and shrugged newly relaxed shoulders.

"Honest to God, is this the best you can do?" one of the women said. "It's awful, is this. There's poor Jean, goodness knows what's happening to her, and you're groping around in the dark."

Now there was group nodding. "Yes, and there's that other woman," David Cooper said.

"What other woman?" Surr wanted to know.

"You know, the dead one. It was on the news at the same time as they said about Jean. Drowned in the canal, wasn't she? And they don't even know who she is."

"Bloody hell. It's pathetic," a small woman in a yellow stretchy onesie muttered. "I didn't see that. Who is she?"

"Like I just said, they don't even know," Cooper said.

The atmosphere in the hall was in danger of becoming nasty. Jordan turned on his phone.

"This has been on the television and in the papers," he said. "I'm surprised you haven't seen the appeals."

"We don't watch the telly now, do we? Nobody does. We just have streaming. All there is on the telly is stupid reality shows or Boris blathering on. Got better things to do," the lady in yellow growled.

"Well okay. This is the person." Jordan opened the image of the woman from the canal.

"They passed around the phone, tutting and clucking."

"Hang on," Surr said. "Let me see that. I don't watch the television, it's depressing and makes me anxious, and the papers are just lies and adverts. Of course, I've been away, as I already said. Let me see that though."

She took the phone and peered at it for a while.

"I could be wrong, I probably am, but isn't this one of the women who used to come to the art classes?"

She looked around at the class who responded with puzzled looks and more shrugged shoulders.

"You know, the life drawing class, the one they had on Tuesdays before the pandemic. In the room at the end. It definitely could be. I think she was one of the models. I saw her in the ladies getting changed one night. You know, she was taking her clothes off and then she just had a dressing gown on. Lily, you were there. We said afterwards how we couldn't do that, standing there in the buff."

"Oh, right. Let me look again."

Jordan glanced at Stella. This was too good to be true, surely. He watched in silence as the two women bent over the screen on his iPhone.

"Yeah. I think you're right. Well, maybe, I wouldn't know her with her clothes on."

There was a guilty giggle from some of them. Surr pursed her lips and sniffed. Lily held the phone nearer.

"I'm not sure. I mean this isn't a nice picture, you can tell she's dead. Oh take it away, I don't want to look at it anymore."

She pushed the phone back to Jordan and gave an exaggerated shudder.

"Who ran the classes?" Stella asked.

"One of the art teachers from the primary school. Don't know her name but the manager will. Actually I think she was retired, but the head of the school might know, either of them should."

Stella and Jordan walked back to the car in silence, Stella was busy on the phone arranging to find the name of the art teacher and Jordan was researching where to find models for life drawing classes. He had found a website with a register. It didn't take him long to realise that he would need to be careful and in fact should probably hand this on to a couple of civilian researchers.

Chapter 45

Back in the incident room Stella hung up the phone and blew out her cheeks. She had spent an hour trying to speak to the head of the primary school who was in lessons, according to her secretary. The manager of the social centre was in hospital and very ill, and a jobsworth at the local education centre, working from home, had refused to provide a list of the students registered for the life drawing classes. It took the threat of a warrant and a report to the papers about intransigence in the face of a murder inquiry before the list was promised.

"Okay, we're waiting for a list of art class students," she said. "Once we have that I want everyone on it. We need to speak to them today. I don't care how. Zoom, Skype, in person, whatever. We want to talk to them about this model. I have been given her details by the tightarse at the education centre and it was like getting blood from a stone. However, her name is Maisie Brewer and she attended the night school; life drawing classes on several occasions. Did the students know her? Had they spent any time with her? When was the last time they saw her? All of that and anything else that comes to mind. I can't believe none of them saw the appeal on the television and recognised her."

"Perhaps they didn't look at her face," John Grice said and then he winced as Jordan turned and glared at him.

"Beneath you, John."

"Yeah, sorry."

"This is the breakthrough we've been looking for," Stella said. "I've got the woman's name and I have an address in Bootle that she gave to the centre. Me and Jordan are going to head down there now."

"Don't they have her NI number if she was working for them?" Grice asked. "That'd help."

"No. It's all a bit casual. The woman I spoke to admitted that they often have trouble finding models so if someone comes along willing to do it, they'll pay them cash in hand if that's what they want. I don't think it's actually a career choice. Not at this level anyway."

"I think I'd rather do bar work," one of the female collators said. "You never know who's going to be looking at you. I mean what checks do they do to make sure everyone is there to draw and paint and not just to ogle?"

"I don't know but now you've raised that, could you find out for me?" Stella said.

* * *

The flat was on the top floor of a red brick terraced house on one of the main roads in Bootle. The door was answered by a man in a greasy white jacket, the logo announced him as working at the nearby Chinese takeaway. He let them in and as Jordan and Stella climbed the dusty flight of stairs, they saw him grab a beanie hat and cotton jacket and leave, dragging his mobile phone from his pocket as he went.

They hammered on the door, but they knew already there wasn't going to be any response, the place had the dead air of 'nobody home'.

"We need the landlord," she said. "I'll get on to the office and have them find the contact details. With luck he'll have a master key. If not, we'll have to get a warrant to enter. In the meantime why don't we go and have a word with that bloke who let us in? The shop was only a couple of doors away."

"I think the takeaway is closed right now but the number is here on the window. From the smell on his clothes I'd say he is working today. I'll give them a ring."

"Nah, sod that. I'm going to hammer on the door. He went off pretty sharpish. I didn't like that."

Stella was back down the stairs and striding along the narrow path in moments and by the time Jordan caught her she was pounding on the wooden surround of a glass door which was festooned with menus, taxi numbers and adverts for rooms to let.

"Ha, would you look at that?" she said. "I reckon we might have found the landlord already."

Chapter 46

A young woman appeared behind the door waving at them to go away. She made the universal sign with her thumb and little finger against the side of her face – '*call on the telephone*'. She pointed to the number on the window. Stella and Jordan had their warrant cards out and pressed against the glass but still she shook her head.

She pointed to her face and covered her chin and mouth with a hand.

"Oh, okay. I get that. She wants us to wear a mask," Jordan said.

"Right, well. I'll have to go back to the car. I've got some in the boot."

"No, here you go." Jordan pulled out one of the ubiquitous blue face coverings in a plastic bag.

Stella held it up to show the woman inside who nodded and moved towards the door. She waited until they were both masked before she let them in and even then scurried behind the counter and pressed back against the wall.

"You have an advert in the window," Jordan said. "Flats to let."

"Yes, my father owns those. What do you want? You don't want a flat."

"No, but are they the ones in the terrace next door?"

"Yes, he owns this whole block, from the hotel up to the car park. But it's all decent, all above board."

"Yes, I'm sure it is. There's nothing to worry about. We're trying to trace a young woman and we think she was one of your tenants. Maybe we could speak to your father?"

"No, he's at home. He is old. He only comes to the shop when it's closed. You can't be in contact with him. If he caught the virus he might die."

"Well, yeah, but we have a job to do," said Stella. She was irritated by the woman's defensiveness.

"Tell you what, you might be able to help. Do you know about the tenants in the flats?" Jordan said.

"I know them. I do the accounts for my father and supervise the cleaning when they move out. All that stuff."

"Oh I thought you worked here, in the takeaway."

"I do, but we all work for the family business. It's for us after all."

"Okay, good. Could you look at this picture and tell us if you recognise this person?"

"Please send that to me. I don't want to touch your phone."

"Oh, for heaven's sake," Stella said.

"It's okay, we can do that. Just give us your email address," Jordan said taking out his phone.

"Please send to the address for orders."

She pointed to the email address on the window. Stella sighed, loudly, but Jordan clicked and scrolled with his thumbs and soon there was the ching of an email arriving.

"Oh yes, that's Maisie. I know her. She lives on the top floor. She's nice."

"At last we're getting there. So, when did you last see her?" Stella said.

The woman behind the counter glanced up and raised an eyebrow. She addressed her response directly to Jordan.

"I haven't seen her for ages. I don't think since the end of the first lockdown. Just once then; she waved to me through the window."

"And you haven't seen her since? You haven't heard from her?" Jordan said.

"No, but that's not unusual. I think she is vegetarian. We do vegetarian but she doesn't buy things from us. We leave the tenants alone if they don't cause any trouble. No need to pester them and they know where we are if they need help."

"What about the rent? Was it paid through a bank by direct debit?" Jordan said.

"I can't tell you about that." The woman shook her head. "You should know about data protection. You have to make a proper application."

As she spoke, she backed away from them towards the curtain-covered door at the back of the shop. She was obviously uncomfortable and unhappy.

"We need access to the flat," Stella said. "Do you have a master key to your properties?"

Before she had finished speaking the woman was shaking her head. "No, no."

"No you don't have a key? If that is the case, then we will get a warrant and we will have a locksmith allow us entry."

"No, I can't go in there. Not in someone else's flat. There might be virus."

"Aw Jesus." Stella put her head in her hands. "Listen, Miss–"

"Tina, I'm Tina."

"Okay, Tina. I am going to tell you this simply. We need access to that flat. We will gain access either with or without your help, but I have to say right here that this is not looking good, and it will be noted in our reports."

"Reports. What reports?"

"Our reports about this case which will be available to all sections of law enforcement. Including HMRC."

They saw the panic light in her eyes and were not surprised at Tina's next words.

"I'll give you the key. You can go in the flat and then put the key through the letterbox after."

"Good enough," Stella said. "But we will still need to speak to you at some point to find out how well you knew Maisie."

"We can do that on Zoom if you like," Jordan said.

"Yes, please. I'll do that," Tina said. "Wait here, I'll get the key."

When she came back, she slid two keys on a simple ring along the counter. There was nothing further to be gained there so they picked it up and let themselves out of the little shop. As they left, Stella looked back through the window to see Tina spraying cleaning liquid on the counter and rubbing at it with a cloth.

"What a bloody wimp," she said. "I mean, talk about over-reaction. I know it's been horrible but if we all behaved like that the country would never get going again."

"Well, I suppose some people are just more scared than others. It's still around and still being passed on," Jordan said.

"I know, but don't we just have to keep going? That woman is still dead, and she still deserves us to find out how and why. Come on, let's get on with it. This has taken too long already. Tell you what though, I could eat a Chinese."

"We'll order one before we leave and pick it up at the door. It might get us back on good terms."

"Good terms my arse. If there's anything dodgy in this flat Miss Tina is going to answer some more questions."

"Hey, come on, a bit of over-reaction there."

Stella looked up at him. "Yeah, sorry. It's just everything. The stupid gossip, the dead end with Tranter, Jean still missing and no clue. I feel such a bloody failure right now."

Chapter 47

Jordan and Stella paused at the door and pulled on shoe covers and gloves. The flat was warm and stuffy. It was small. A narrow entrance hall opened into a square living room with a window overlooking the road. A small wooden table was beneath the window and two dining chairs with faded cushioned seats were placed underneath it.

A two-seater bed settee was in the middle of the floor facing the wall where a television had been mounted above a set of shelves. There were coloured cushions ranged along the back of the sofa and in the small easy chair. It was dusty but neat and cheerful. On the walls were prints of fashion show posters – Paris, London, New York – and in the corner was a pile of glossy magazines. Jordan took a pen from his pocket and lifted them carefully at the edges. *Vogue*, *Elle*, British *Vogue*, *Glamour*, *Harper's Bazaar*. Some of them were old but the ones on the top were recent issues.

"I guess we know what she was into then," Stella said. "Just a quick shuftie and then we'll get the scene of crime people in. Doesn't look as though there's been a break in or anything, so I guess she wasn't taken from here. Let's just have a glance at the rest of it."

"I'll have a look at the bedroom, do you want to do the kitchen and bathroom?"

"Yeah, sounds good."

They met again by the front door.

"All neat in the bedroom but there is a laptop in there. We'll get SOC to bag it and tag it. That could be a gold mine," Jordan said.

"The kitchen is neat and tidy, lots of health food stuff in the cupboards. The fridge did have salad and veggies in it but now it absolutely honks, and it's mostly just slime with bits in. Yuk."

"So she's been gone a while. I'm looking forward to having a look at her laptop."

"I've called in the circus. Ha, that won't please Miss Tina, I'll bet. Now, back to base I reckon and see if they've had any luck with the two blokes on the canal bank."

"When we first talked about Jean being seen out for her walk, we said it was a very tenuous link, do you remember?" Jordan said.

"Yeah, and now it's a fair bit stronger. We do at least know that at some time there was the chance that they were in the same place."

"The yoga class didn't all know Maisie though, did they?"

"No, not as far as they were letting on anyway," Stella said.

"They should have had some interviews with the life drawing students by now. I know these are tiny steps, but they are steps forward and at least we've identified the poor woman. Someone is going to have to inform her family, as soon as we trace them."

"I hate doing that, but I guess it's down to me."

"I can do it if you like," Jordan said.

"No, you're alright. It's my job, isn't it? Mind, if you want to come along, I won't say no."

"Yep. Let's do that."

As they drove back to Copy Lane Jordan called Mel.

"Is there news?" she asked.

"No, nothing new really. I'm sorry. How are you holding up?"

He heard her start to cry. "What's awful, Jordan, is that I forget. When I'm working, I'm totally focused, I have to be, and I forget. Then I have a break, or it gets to the end of my shift, and it hits me all over again. Every day, over and over it hits me again."

"I'm so sorry. We are doing everything we can."

"I'm sure you are but it's not working, is it?"

He didn't have an answer for her and defaulted to the reason for his call.

"Listen Mel, this is going to sound odd but it's just one of the leads we're following up."

"Okay, go ahead."

"Did Jean ever go to art classes?"

"How do you mean?"

"Night school, life drawing particularly."

"What, you mean nudes?"

"That sort of thing, yes."

"Jesus no. She'd die of embarrassment. Why do you want to know?"

"It's nothing. It was just a chance, don't worry about it."

"Okay. But no, nothing ever like that."

His phone rang again immediately. At the note of enthusiasm in his voice Stella glanced across, eyes wide. She watched him go from hope to dull acceptance and she was already prepared when he signed off and shook his head.

"It was Kath."

"Okay. And?"

"Found the bloke who saw Jean on her walk."

"It's not good, is it?"

"Well, it's nothing really. He rang in to confirm he had seen her. Definitely her, he reckons. Thing is he'd been visiting a lady friend."

"By that you mean a fancy woman."

"Pretty much, yes. It's his bit on the side and that's why he didn't want to give his name. Conscience got the better of him in the end. Kath has double-checked with the woman, only on the phone but it all seems kosher. She wants to know if we want to bring him in."

"What do you reckon?"

"It seems unfair to me. He'd probably have to explain to his wife, it could cause him all sorts of trouble and at the end of the day he was being a good citizen."

"Apart from the dodgy nooky – yeah. I guess we'll leave it for now. Poor bloke's probably sweating cobs already – I guess that'll teach him."

"Maybe."

Chapter 48

"Can we all just stop what we're doing for a mo? I reckon it's best to bring everyone up to date as quick as we can. After that you'll all have a chance to chime in if there's anything to contribute. I want to hear about the art class particularly. We've heard from Kath about our witness and his extracurricular activities so what else have we got?"

As she organised the team and brought things together, Jordan felt reassured that he'd made the right decision letting Stella keep control. Okay there would be a reckoning, so be it. For now this was the best thing for the case. Everyone was working well and there was no resentment. In all closed communities, perceived slights and insults could be blown out of all proportion and he would try to sell that when he had the inevitable conversation with his bosses. He had a couple of days while DCI Martin was tied up with his meetings. He could delay the showdown with DCI Griffiths by simply feeding back information as if he was running the show. They were doing it together. It was good enough.

Stella told them about the flat and that it was unlikely that Maisie had been taken from there.

"If she was, I think she must have gone willingly. We didn't see any sign of disturbance. Anyway the technicians are in there now and just knowing who she is, where she was, is a huge move forward."

John Grice stood and moved to the front of the room.

"We've spoken to all the art students that we could find. The class was run by a retired teacher, and she has now gone to Spain to live with her sister. We're trying to contact her but it's not as easy as it used to be. We'll do what we can. I have tried to email her, but the message came back as undeliverable so obviously the address is defunct.

"Apart from that not many people remembered our victim. We have asked the ones who kept their work to send us anything that they think shows Maisie. I don't know how much that will help except to confirm she was there. They didn't talk to the models particularly and didn't know much about them. From what they said, this teacher was strict and kept them all working. Maisie didn't come through an agency, unfortunately, and was used on a casual basis.

"There was one woman, a… erm" – he consulted his notes – "Mrs Harwood, she seems to have spoken to Maisie a bit. They walked to the station together a couple of times. She remembered her saying she was hoping to become a model. Apparently, London was the ultimate aim. She was doing casual bar work but didn't say where. A bit of modelling but again didn't give details. She gave the impression she was taking anything that came up, hence the art classes. She was very upset when it looked as if all that was about to dry up. Mrs Harwood said she became very emotional wondering how she would cope but that was that. There were no more classes after that, and they didn't keep in touch."

"We'll have another word with her, there might be something there. Is that it?" Stella said.

"Just about. We've traced her next of kin from the form she filled in for the art class but it's not much help. I've sent you the details."

Stella read through the information she'd been sent about Maisie Brewer and sighed loudly.

"She only had one relative as far as they could ascertain, a grandmother in Glasgow who was in long-term elderly care. Kath had spoken directly to the care home and been told that Mrs Brewer was unlikely to understand that her granddaughter had been killed. She couldn't remember enough of her past to be of any help and anyway wasn't able to hold a proper conversation most of the time."

"We still have to go through the motions," Jordan said. "John, can you contact someone from Police Scotland and have them send a family liaison officer round there to make sure things are as bad as they say? Doesn't seem as though there is any point in us going up there."

He stood in front of the whiteboard and paced back and forth for a while longer.

"Kath," he said to the detective constable, "get on to the digital forensic department. Find out if they've got the laptop from the flat in Bootle. I'm really keen to find out what there is on it." He turned to Stella who had come to stand beside him. "I'm going to go through the responses from Jean's appeal, we might have missed something."

"Good idea. I'll bring the reports up to date and then I'll get on to that as well. Unless anything comes up. I expect I should copy Dave in with the report?"

"Erm, no. I need to speak to him anyway. I'll do that. Just send me a copy, yeah?"

"Okay. No probs. Give him my regards."

Chapter 49

When you don't know what you are looking for it's easy to miss something, so Jordan settled down with a mug of coffee and began to review the notes the team had made. There weren't as many as he had hoped and especially the response to the second appeal had been disappointing. Apart from the man who had seen Jean out walking, and that had proved to be disappointing too. They had attached quite a lot of importance to her being seen by the canal. At least they could be pretty sure now that it was true, so that was one positive.

It looked as though she had walked the empty streets alone and had been seen by only that one man until she arrived back at her house safely, as far as they could tell. Throughout the day and evening no-one reported seeing suspicious characters around or strange visitors. But then almost everyone had been indoors during the wet afternoon and evening.

However, when he picked up the report from a teenager in the Old Roan and began to read, the hairs on Jordan's arms prickled as chills ran up and down his skin. The youngster had been missed in the first round of house-to-house visits. He'd been, according to his mother, 'Away staying at a mate's but he won't have seen anything anyway – never looks up from that bloody computer, unless it's to squint at his phone.' But she'd had to eat her words when they saw the second appeal and he told her about the night he ordered pizza, late and unbeknownst to his parents. He had peered out of the window when he heard a motor, because he didn't want a ring on the doorbell. He thought it had been the delivery but it was a white van parked in the dark, wet road. He hadn't been interested; his food wasn't in there after all. But when the delivery did arrive, and he had scurried to collect his supper before the rest of the house was disturbed, the driver of the van was in the side drive of Jean Barker's house.

"Stella, I reckon we're going to the Old Roan. John, call this young bloke, Andy Fox, tell him we need to speak to him and if he's not at home find out where he is and tell him to either get back to his house or come in here. The details are in the phone interview record. I've sent you the reference number."

"Did I take it, boss?" he asked.

"I think it was one of yours."

"Have I missed something? Shit, have I?"

"Don't worry about it now, we'll see whether it goes anywhere, but don't worry, just get me a meeting with this lad."

They heard him cursing under his breath as he scrolled through the list. "Oh shit, boss. I'm sorry. I've cocked up, haven't I?"

"Not the time right now, John, just let's make it right."

Jordan was aware of sideways glances from other people, but this wasn't a time to think about the young detective's feelings. There would be time later for recriminations and soul-searching. For now they just had to find out if this was going to go anywhere. It didn't seem much, just a chance observation, but it could be very important indeed.

Chapter 50

Andy Fox tried hard to be cool and dismissive, but his hands shook a little as he raised the glass of cola to drink.

"We are really hoping you can help us here, Andy," Jordan said. "There's nothing to be worried about."

"Not worried, am I? Just don't like the bizzies round my gaff, like."

As they were sitting in his mother's neat living room on a pink velour sofa the description of his 'gaff' had Jordan struggling to hold back a grin.

"Well, we'll try not to keep you too long. Do you mind if we record this? It's just for our own records and it'll be deleted as soon as we've finished with it."

Andy gave a brief nod. He leaned back on the sofa and propped his feet on the coffee table. His mother, watching through a serving hatch from the kitchen, coughed. He huffed and placed his feet back on the floor.

"So, most importantly can you tell us what time you ordered the pizza, and what time it was delivered?" Jordan said.

Andy glanced up at his mum. It was obvious that he was more worried about the repercussions of ordering unapproved snacks than possibly seeing a crime out of the window.

"Late. I was hungry, like. I'd been doing my homework."

"Yes, of course you were," his mother muttered. "Think I was born yesterday? Homework my arse."

"Well, anyway. I was hungry so I just ordered a meat feast and some garlic bread."

"Bloody garlic bread stinking up the bedroom. You've been told."

"Mrs Fox, I think this will be much quicker if Andy just tells us what happened and then we can leave you in peace," Stella said.

The woman turned away from the serving hatch and began slamming dishes into the dishwasher.

"Andy, do you know what time it was?" Jordan asked.

"Hang on. I'll look on my phone." Thumbs flying across the little screen, it took moments and Andy turned his phone to show Jordan an order record on his Pizza Hut account.

"So two in the morning and the pizza was delivered by Just Eat?"

"Yep. I heard the car and I thought, f–" He cut of the expletive and glanced at the serving hatch. "I just thought, that was quick, but when I looked out it was a van over the road. Anyway, when the pizza bloke showed up, the van was still there. I thought it was odd because it was late, like. Anyway I saw the bloke was in the side passage. Standing by the fence."

"And then what happened?" Jordan asked.

"I had my pizza."

"You didn't do anything about the man at the house across the road?"

"How d'ya mean?"

"Well, you didn't tell anyone, or watch to see what happened?"

"I had my pizza. I didn't want it to go cold, did I?"

"So, you just went back to your room?"

"Yeah. Not my business, like."

Jordan swallowed a sigh. "Okay, Andy. So what can you tell me about the van and the driver?"

"How d'ya mean?"

"Do you know what make it was?" It was obvious there was no point talking about registration numbers. As a witness Andy Fox wasn't going to win any gold stars, but anything he could tell them was more than they had before.

"Oh, right. It was a VW Caddy."

"Okay. You seem very sure about that?"

"Yeah, that's what it was. A white one. My uncle's got one. I did wonder, like, whether it was him at first." Andy glanced up. "I wondered if his bird had chucked him out again. Always happening and then he turns up here and I thought, oh shit not again. I have to share my room with him, and he farts in his sleep. It stinks."

"Andy!"

The shout from the kitchen made him grin.

"Well he does, Mam. Anyway it wasn't him, was it?"

"Can you tell us anything about the driver? Anything at all would be brilliant," Stella said.

"He wasn't very big. Just normal size, not as big as him." He pointed at Jordan. "He was just ordinary. He had a jacket on with the hood up. Course I couldn't see what colour or nothing because the lights were all out at the house. It was dark, like."

"What did he do?" Jordan asked.

"He didn't do nothing. He stood by the fence just watching and then I went in, cos of my pizza."

"Okay. Will you come down to the station in Copy Lane and give us a written statement? It won't take long."

"If I have to. Is she dead then, that woman?"

"We hope not," Jordan said, "but we are worried about her."

"I expect she is. Probably chopped up and in wheelie bins."

"Andrew!"

The shout from the kitchen told them it was probably time to leave. As they walked down the narrow front path, they could hear Andy being read the riot act.

"It's not much but at least we have an accurate time and, more importantly, a vehicle to look out for," Jordan said.

"Thank heavens for Andy's uncle."

"Yes, and his angry 'bird'. Right, I'll send all that back and we can start looking for our little VW van. I suppose there's only a couple of million of them around so that shouldn't take long. We need to contact Just Eat and have a chat with the delivery driver from that night. He might have seen something, if we're lucky."

Chapter 51

Back in the station everyone's head was down over their screens.

"I know there are dozens of little white vans," Jordan said, "but we have the time and the location so it's not impossible. Anyone who can stay late, please do. I'll send out for pizza."

There was a muted cheer.

"Pizza Hut, I reckon. Under the circumstances," he said to Stella.

"Got to be. My shout though, eh?"

He was going to argue but it was traditionally the SIO who paid for this stuff, so he held his peace.

There was a message on his computer from David Griffiths asking him to call into St Anne Street as soon as he could. He read the email without opening it. He knew the DCI would have a delivery notification and possibly a read notice as well. They had perhaps a couple of days and then he was going to have to face the music and admit he'd ignored orders. They could conceivably throw the book at him. They could suspend him. Just when things were beginning to move. He said a silent prayer to Nana Gloria's god who he didn't really believe in, but he promised he'd go with her to church next time he went down there, providing he was left alone for now.

Kath came and stood beside his desk.

"Couple of things, boss. The delivery driver from Just Eat doesn't remember seeing the van or the bloke. He has a record of the delivery but can't actually remember it. 'Just another Pizza' is what he said."

"Did he have a dashcam?"

"Afraid not. He's supposed to but…" She shrugged.

"Okay, that seems to be par for the course with this case. What else was there?"

"John asked me to get on to Police Scotland. They sent a couple of officers round to see Maisie's granny. Apparently, it was pretty bad. She's away with the fairies. But the coppers were on the ball, and they sent us some images of the room. I sent them through to your machine. There are pictures of Maisie all over the place and some of them look like professional shots. She wrote to her granny a bit. They're forwarding copies of the letters. The carers read them to the old woman, but they don't reckon she understood. However, they do seem to bear out what we've been told. She was doing bits and pieces of jobs and still hoping to get to London for modelling work. The address on them is the flat in Bootle. Plus, the latter ones did seem quite hopeful, and she mentions a meeting. No details but there are no letters after that, and they had no calls from her. It could give us a timeline."

"Excellent. Really great. As soon we have those let me have a look at them."

"On it, boss."

That was the second time he'd been addressed as the SIO. Was he giving the impression that he was in charge even though he had tried not to? Did it really matter now that things were moving and they might solve this? Whether they would solve it in time to bring Jean Barker home was another matter.

Chapter 52

At first there was an air of subdued excitement. The pizza came but nobody stopped work to eat, they placed the greasy slices on paper plates and napkins and chewed as they scrolled and scanned. Surely it wouldn't take them long. They had the time and type of van.

Locally there was the M57, the M58 and the A59 all converging on the junction of Switch Island where a couple of minor roads also joined the confluence. There were a number of vans of the right size and various makes, and allowing for a possible error on behalf of the witness they were all followed. Each time one was spotted a flurry of interest would go around the group. Each time they would be traced onward either towards Southport, towards the city or to Wales, the Wirral, and beyond. None were seen entering the residential areas around the Old Roan. None were seen leaving.

They allowed for stoppages on the way and they allowed for diversions, thus they searched for hours either side of the narrow time frame given them by Andy Fox. There were no private CCTV cameras in the roads around Jean's house. The first one was at the Asda Superstore, and they couldn't find the van there or passing the railway station or the retail park.

* * *

After three hours Stella sent them all home. "We can start again tomorrow. I know it's frustrating, but you can only do this for so long."

For a while Jordan and Stella sat in the quiet incident room, tired and disheartened.

"He could be wrong, that Andy. He could have got the time and the day wrong," Stella said.

"Nope, not unless he buys pizza every night. We saw the record on his Pizza Hut page and the Just Eat driver had a record even though he didn't actually remember it."

"Oh, yeah. So where did it go? It can't have just vaporised. I suppose she could have been put into another vehicle. Of course this is always assuming he took her away."

"If he didn't, then where is she? We've searched the whole area by now and there's no sign of her. If he killed her or even just struggled with her in the house then there was no evidence of it; that's impossible. So, no, he took her out. The only thing we have is the broken plant pot and forensically what they found in the kitchen, a couple of spots of blood which could have been there for a while. He can hardly have gone further in, or they would have found something else: hair, fingerprints, signs of a struggle. So, he grabbed her either from the step, hence the flowerpot, or just inside," Jordan said. "Maybe she opened the door to him. That indicates that she may have known him."

"You're right, it's the only explanation. But then why was he standing in the dark side passage. Where did he go? You know, maybe he didn't really go anywhere."

"How do you mean?"

"We've assumed he kidnapped her and took her right away," Stella said. "What if he didn't do that? What if he didn't actually go very far at all? Not even onto the main roads. Tomorrow, I reckon we arrange to launch a new search, bigger and more in depth. We need to look in all the sheds and garages."

"But if we go down that route, we have to start a house-to-house; attics, basements and all of that."

"We would have done that already if she'd been a kid."

"You're right," Jordan said. "Why didn't we see this before?"

"I don't see that there is any other answer. That van didn't disappear into thin air so it's there, it's still nearby. That's the first thing we should do, we can get on to that immediately. We'll organise a visual search for a van like that in the streets around her house."

Chapter 53

Jordan hardly slept and it was just coming up to six when he turned on the lights in the incident room. The place still smelled of pizza and stale bodies. The door opened and a bloke with a cleaner's trolley stuck his head in.

"Alright, mate, just getting to this one. Do you want me to come back later, or what?"

"No, it's fine. I'll go down to the canteen and get some breakfast. Sorry about the mess, we were working late last night."

"No probs, I'll be as quick as I can. Is that her then?" He pointed at the image of Jean on the noticeboard.

"Yes, that's our missing woman."

"Poor cow."

"Yes."

"Well, I don't suppose you'll find her now."

Why did everyone assume the worst? In truth, he knew why. It had been too long. Jordan thought of Mel working in Manchester and holding on to hope that she knew must be more and more forlorn as each hour passed. At some stage the hope of finding Jean would become a desperate desire to simply know the truth. He sighed and walked down the quiet corridor to the canteen. His appetite had gone and the coffee in the incident room was better than the stewed drink on offer there. He turned away and went to the back door where he gazed out at the half-empty car park until he judged it would be okay to go back to his desk.

The call from Stella came through just before seven.

"Jordan, I'm in the shit."

"What's happened?"

"I've got the bloody virus. I felt rotten yesterday but I thought I was just tired, but I've done one of those tests today and it's positive. Oh bloody hell, I've probably given it to everybody. What am I going to do?"

"Don't panic. You sound awful. Listen, there's nothing you can do, nothing at all. We've all been vaccinated, and we'll just wait and see. Go to bed. I'll let you know if anything happens. This is not your fault, Stella. You've just joined the millions of others."

"But what about the case, what about Jean?"

"We'll just keep on. I'll organise the searches we discussed and let you know what happens. Nothing you can do."

He went to the locker room and took the test kit from his bag. He gave it the full fifteen minutes, but it was negative. Okay, he might be okay, he might not. For now he had to just keep on going. He was trying not to acknowledge the quisling thought in the back of his mind. If he handled this properly it would solve the problem with Griffiths. The idea that Stella's illness could be a benefit shamed him, but it was true, nevertheless. He stuffed the cardboard box back in his locker. Right, so he would solve this now. He would solve it and make sure that at the end of the day Stella got the credit she deserved for her part in it all. It was all he could do.

Chapter 54

DCI Martin was still out of his office. Jordan left a message with Karen and then gave the news to the rest of the team.

"You'd better all do a test and take whatever action's necessary," he said. "Otherwise we are going to do a house-to-house search for Jean Barker. Wear your masks."

There was a quiet murmur. John Grice raised his hand.

"We've done a search though, haven't we?"

"We have, but only in the public spaces. It was in the early days when we thought that maybe she had gone off and become confused or been injured. Now we know pretty much for certain that she's been taken, and we didn't find that van. So, the thinking is she's locked in a shed, garage, basement, and waiting for us to find her, or, and I admit that it's probably more likely at this stage, her body is hidden away somewhere. Now, if it is the latter, we still have to find her. She deserves that, as does her daughter."

Martin called mid-morning to say that he was still waiting for a conversation about the running of the case, but as things seemed to be moving along then he'd call around and see how many extra bodies could be found to help.

"I reckon a board at the station and the superstore would help. Glad to see you have taken hold of this. I'm getting all sorts of hassle from up top." He wanted to know about the other case, the one that he insisted on calling the 'big' investigation.

Jordan tried to convince him that the two were linked but even as he recited the connections, he knew they sounded feeble and could tell that the DCI wasn't fully on board, but not willing to get into it remotely.

"We'll talk next week when I'm back. If you speak to Stella, give her my best – I bloody hope she hasn't infected the whole station." With that he rang off.

There was no point Jordan going to Old Roan now. The place would be crawling with uniformed officers and community support bods. He knew that the right place for him was in the office directing things.

He sent Stella an email asking if she was well enough to look at the letters Maisie had sent to her grandmother.

She rang him. "Course I am, just a bit wobbly, I'm taking painkillers and chewing my fingernails off here. Send them over, please – and anything else I can help with."

The incident room was almost empty, but Kath was still at her desk.

"Are you okay?" Jordan asked, from a distance.

"I'm fine. I've already had it so I'm not in much danger for now. I'm not much use in a house-to-house though. I'm waiting for a knee replacement. Been over a year already and still no sign. I can't walk for too long. I'm not wasting time though. I've got Google Earth here and I'm scanning for white vans parked out of the way and then contacting the others so they can make sure they look. Of course the images are not live but people that have those vehicles often keep them for a while so if there was one two or three years ago, chances are they'll still have them."

"Great idea, thanks. Let me know if anything unusual pops up."

"Will do, boss."

Throughout the day there were reports of likely vehicles found. These were followed for the most part by either frustrating delays before they could speak to the owners, or an interview that cleared the drivers of any suspicion. As the estate was swamped with officers there was the expected kickback. People who didn't want their premises searched, some who outright refused and some who harassed the officers even when they understood who it was they were looking for. A refusal didn't mean guilt but each one was noted for later examination.

By nine at night they had all had enough. Jordan called a halt and told everyone to be prepared to be back at it the following day. The responses were not exactly enthusiastic, but he knew they would keep at it, there was no other choice.

Before he left for the night, he rang Mel in Manchester and told her what they were doing. He didn't want her to hear about it on social media.

"You think she's dead, don't you?" Mel sobbed through the phone.

"I don't know, Mel, I honestly don't, but we are doing all that we can."

'Doing all that we can' – it felt too little, too late.

Chapter 55

It had been a long day. Jordan dragged his jacket from the back of his chair and stuffed his phone into the pocket. He picked up his laptop bag and turned away from the desk. There was never any question that he would ignore the internal call that rang right then, but he groaned as he lifted the receiver.

"DI Carr, Steve from forensics. We've managed to get into that laptop belonging to Maisie Brewer. I'll send over the report as soon as, but I was told you were waiting to hear."

"Brilliant, go on."

It was much as they had expected, social media, streaming services, and emails to modelling agencies.

Jordan made a few notes, but he knew it would all be itemised in the report.

"What about Facebook?"

The technician gave a grunt. Most youngsters used something else, Snapchat, WhatsApp, Instagram and one of the dozens of others depending on just what they were doing.

"Her social media presence was less than a lot of people her age. So, either it just didn't float her boat, or she didn't have much time," he said.

She had used the direct messaging application of Facebook to keep in touch with some friends she'd had since school. Three of them were still based in Scotland and cheering her on in her efforts to get to the big city and start her modelling career.

> *Keep trying Maz you'll do it.*
> *Ur gorjus u r.*
>
> *Feeling a bit down just had a refusal from another agent.*
>
> *Don't get down pal. It will happen 4 u.*
>
> *I need my hair cutting and I've got no ££*
>
> *R U still working at the pub?*
>
> *No, finished. Asked the landlord if I cud work in the takeaway but no go.*

And so it went on for weeks, her friends offering support and Maisie see-sawing between hope and despair until the final messages.

> *Got an interview, sent my portfolio – YAY*

Brill. Where at?

Don't want to say
Don't want to jinx it.
But it's a really unexpected contact.
Just shows you that you never know.

Aw— oh well gud luck. Tell us what happens.

There was nothing after that anywhere. No images posted, no further contact with anyone. At first the friends had messaged her, excited and waiting for news. A couple of days later a few messages of patience and sympathy telling her that if it hadn't worked out, they were there for her. These continued for a while and then eventually petered out. So, at least now they had an idea when she was taken. If she hadn't been so superstitious, they could have had so much more.

"Shame you haven't got her phone. She did have the Find My Device app and we gave it a go but there was nothing. It's a pity," Steve said.

"Tell me about it," Jordan said. "Why would the searching app not work?"

"Could be that the battery is flat. The phone could be in a dead zone, or she could even have turned off the location tracker. Of course it could just be that the thing is smashed and discarded, SIM thrown in the canal where she was found. No way to tell really, shame though."

"Still, thanks so much, Steve, that's brilliant. Have you finished with the laptop now?"

"God no, we're going to get you the addresses of those women in Scotland. Even though you haven't got her phone, chances are they might have spoken to her, texted or whatever, so no, we're not done with it yet, not by a long chalk."

It was a bit late, but he couldn't resist calling Stella.

"I've made sure they'll copy you in. Maybe if you feel up to it you can contact the friends. We could ask Police Scotland to do it, but I reckon it'll be more valuable if we speak to them directly."

"Yeah, I'll do that."

"How are you feeling?"

"Bloody rotten now. It doesn't help that the place is such a mess and now the workmen have gone because they don't want to risk catching anything. I'm okay though. My mate from upstairs is getting shopping and he's even left food so I'll be fine. I just hope you haven't got it. We'll be really in the shit then. What will we do?"

"I'm okay right now, don't look for trouble. Just get better, yeah?"

He put a hand to his forehead. Was his throat a bit rough? Jordan shook his head. He was fine, he had to be fine. Jean could still be out there. He didn't have any option but to be fine.

Chapter 56

The troops were out early. It wasn't such a huge area, but it was very built-up. People who had been out the day before had responded to the messages pushed through the door and suggested times when they would be at home. It was going well but it had achieved nothing, except they knew where Jean wasn't.

Jordan made himself and Kath coffee. She was still viewing the Google Earth images.

"I've been feeding this information back to the guys on the ground. It's of limited use, I know that. Some of the images are quite old now, but as I said if anyone had a van, it's worth looking to see if they still have one. I'm not looking at houses because they only have front drives or little garages. I'm scanning the schools and there's a sports centre and a couple of builders' yards. I'll be honest though, sir, I'm sort of giving up hope. I thought it was a good idea but now I'm not so sure and I'm pretty much done."

"It was worth giving it a go. Did you find any that the officers on the ground hadn't seen?"

"A couple, yes."

"Okay so it was worth a shot."

"I guess so. Look, that one" – she pointed at the screen – "that was there when the image was taken, and the lads went round but now he has a bigger van and a different colour. So, I feel pretty useless now. I find it really frustrating. I was going to take some painkillers and maybe go out there for an hour. I reckon it'd be more worthwhile."

"Tell you what, Stella is pretty rough this morning, I called her on my way in. Why don't you take these numbers? Send her a text to let her know you're going to do it. Give her a break?"

He gave her the contact details for Maisie's friends and explained that the young women were probably unaware of what had happened to Maisie.

"All they will know is that she has stopped contacting them. They could be a bit miffed with her, think she got the job and has gone off to London and dropped them. Do you think you can handle it? We need to know whether she told any of them where she was going, who she was seeing. You know the sort of thing. Get on to that for now. It'll give you a break from the screen at least."

He could tell that she was disappointed that the idea hadn't been of more use. A drone would be perfect to do in real time what Kath had been forced to do using old images. It wasn't happening though, unless they could find someone in the force who had one. The idea took root in his head, and he made a couple of calls. The tech department seemed like the place but in the end it went nowhere. There would be too many hoops to jump through just on the off chance that they would spot something.

Back at his desk he logged on to Google Earth and put in Jean Barker's address. He was convinced that she was there, somewhere; either Jean or her remains were waiting to be found. He zoomed in on the addresses they had visited.

"Kath," he called over to where she was making notes. "Did you see the van in the school, the one where the yoga class is?"

"I did. It's not there now. They even spoke to the head about it, but she didn't know anything. She wasn't there when the picture was taken."

"It's in a yard at the back. What about the caretaker, did anyone ask him about it?"

"No, don't believe so. He's off, not been in since early on in the week."

"Do we have his address?"

They didn't and within minutes Jordan was on the phone speaking to the school secretary who gave him the usual spiel about data protection.

"I don't want to have to go through the palaver of applying for a warrant and I really need to talk to him urgently. So, if you could see your way clear…"

She made him seethe a little while longer until she eventually gave him the information. People usually did in the end, and it was as if they needed to protest so that later on they could claim that they were threatened, bullied or whatever. He tried the landline and the mobile and there was no answer to either, not even a voice mailbox. He felt the prickle on the back of his neck, the one that told him things were falling into place, the one that had led him into trouble before. He called John Grice, gave him the address, and arranged to meet him.

Chapter 57

The flat was above a parade of shops. As Jordan and John Grice parked in front of the shopping centre, a group of young people on bikes sped past, heads down, hoods up.

"What do we know about this area?" Jordan asked.

"It was mostly built in the sixties. Council houses for the workers at the new factories. It was okay for a while but now the factories have gone, and the houses are mostly either private or private landlords. It's seen better days, I think it's fair to say," Grice said.

"Come on, this flat is above the shops in the square. Access round the back."

"What about the van, though?" Grice asked.

"Good point. Is there parking here, apart from for the shopping?"

Grice looked at his tablet. "There are some garages down at the end. Don't know if they're allocated to the shops or what."

"Get on to the station, have someone find out. This is the flat."

They tried the small plastic bell push but it made no sound. They hammered on the door and were met with silence. Jordan walked along the narrow concrete walkway to peer through the grubby window.

"Kitchen," he said. "No sign of anyone around. I'm going to arrange for a warrant. This set-up is ringing all sorts of bells."

"Ha, not this one though, eh?" Grice pointed at the door.

"Very funny. I met this bloke, back at the yoga centre. Not the friendliest of people but there was nothing about him that made me suspicious. Now though, there's something, isn't there? Okay let's go down and have a nose around the garages."

There was a small, terraced block of prefabricated concrete storage units. They were big enough for one car or a small van and not much else. There were no windows, and the roller shutter doors were all closed and padlocked.

As they turned away a car swung into the little access road. The driver flashed his lights in warning as they stepped aside. He pulled in front of one of the units and clambered out. Jordan held up his warrant card as he walked towards the vehicle.

"Could I have a word, mate?"

"Do I have a choice?"

"Of course. But I just need to know if you are acquainted with Mr Beetham, Brian?"

"Acquainted, eh? Well, I don't know about that. I know who you mean. Seen him down the pub now and then. Wouldn't say I was acquainted. Anyway, that's his lock-up if you're asking. He lives in one of the flats in the square."

"Have you seen him recently?"

"No, nothing odd in that though. We don't mix particularly."

"Any reason for that?"

"Not really, he's just not my type of person."

"Can you explain what you mean?"

"No. If you don't know, I'm not going to tell you. We're all different and each to his own. Not my sort. Don't know anything about him, don't want to, and now I have to get on or my missus'll be less than pleased. I've got the fish for tea."

"Thanks."

"Yeah, you're welcome. 'Acquainted', ha!"

"Just before you go. Do you know what sort of a car he drives?"

"Not a car. Some clapped-out old van. Had it years. I don't think he's got much money. He's a caretaker or something. Don't think it pays that well. Anyway, as I say – fish."

He held up a white plastic bag and turned to open the door to his garage.

Chapter 58

"What now, boss?" Grice asked as they walked past the betting office and the pawn shop.

"We wait here for the warrant, I guess. In the meantime, I'll update my notes. Take your car round the back and keep an eye on the flat. I don't think he'll come back but you never know."

"What do you make of it all?"

"I'm trying to get my head around it. It's not much more than just a feeling. Well, a bit more than that. We know all three of them spent time at the community centre. I imagine he's there pretty much full time so there's a good chance that he's come into contact with both of them. All we can do is get into his place and have a hunt around. There could be some answers in there."

Jordan's phone rang. Grice raised a hand and went to his own car.

"Kath, what have you got for me?" Jordan said.

"Have you a minute to talk?"

"Go ahead."

She had been in touch with all three women in Scotland. They had been shocked and tearful when they were told about Maisie. They had tried to keep in touch and one of them – Jane Harper – had even visited the granny in her care home.

"Of course that did no good," Kath said.

"Did they just leave it then? What, write her off and carry on with their lives?" Jordan asked.

They hadn't. Jane had been the forceful one and she had encouraged them to keep trying to contact Maisie. No answer to the phone which eventually didn't even ring. In the end she visited her local police station.

"There was nothing on HOLMES," Jordan said.

"No. This is not good. Apparently, the officer on the desk told her they could do nothing because Maisie wasn't a child, and they had no reason to be concerned for her. He said she was outside the jurisdiction of Police Scotland anyway and he advised her to just keep trying to contact her. She said he was very condescending and pretty much insinuated that she should get over it and accept that her mate had dumped them because something better had come along."

"Bloody hell. He didn't make a record?"

"Apparently not, boss."

"So, no idea who this numpty was? Christ."

"It'll be really difficult to find out. We'd need to be able to establish when she went to the station and then find out who was on duty. It's too long ago, I reckon, and all too difficult when in reality it isn't going to be of any help to anyone. Once the poor lass's fate is known nobody is going to admit to such a screw-up anyway."

"If he'd done his job properly there might have been a chance to find her, maybe even save her."

"I know. What do you want me to do now, boss? If you want me to take it further, I will."

"Put all that into a report. It won't do any good now, but we need to have a record of it. You're right, it's of no help, but let's make sure it's noted. I'm assuming Maisie didn't tell any of her friends who she was seeing for this so-called appointment."

"No. Perhaps she really didn't hold out much hope. She could have just been putting on a brave face, so they didn't know her true situation, you know with the nude modelling and what have you, so she kept it to herself."

A message arrived on Jordan's phone. "Okay, my warrant has come through. Listen, as a priority get as many of the team as possible finding out everything there is to know about Brian Beetham. You're doing a great job, Kath."

"Aw, thanks, boss."

Jordan finished his call and walked across the precinct.

The lock gave way after two or three thumps from John Grice's shoulder. They could have waited to gain access, but Jordan was seething with impatience and annoyance at the missed opportunity to trace Maisie.

"Call the station and arrange for a locksmith to make this place secure when we've finished."

The flat was chilly inside. It was tidy but sparsely furnished with a cheap three-piece suite and a chipboard table, there was a small radio but no television. The cupboards in the kitchen were mostly bare. Just a few tins of soup and beans. A loaf in the fridge was already past the use-by date and the cheese was hard and mould rimmed the edges.

Jordan was examining the fitted cupboards in the living room when John Grice called through from the other end of the narrow hallway.

"Boss, I reckon we need to call in the tech lads."

Jordan found him in the tiny box room overlooking the back alleyway. The windows were covered with a roller blind. There was no bed in this room. An L-shaped desk wound around the corner with a swivel chair in front of it. There were three PCs, a keyboard, mouse, and expensive-looking earphones. There were three big screens connected to the machines and against another wall a bank of shelves holding equipment that looked familiar but neither of them could readily name.

"This is quite a set-up for someone who's short of money," Jordan said.

His fingers itched to switch on the machines, but he held back.

"Okay, forget the locksmith," he said. "We need to have the experts on this. It's impossible to know what sort of protection he has on it so let's just call in the SOC and technical department. We need to search this flat and the garage. I'll wait to speak to the technicians, and you get back to the station. We need an all-points alert out on his van. You get on to DVLA now we have his address and move this along. We're getting somewhere, I can feel it. We need to find this guy as soon as possible."

Chapter 59

Steve from the digital department was first to arrive. He entered the room wearing a white paper suit and gloves, foot covers and a face mask. He raised his eyebrows at Jordan who had gloves and shoe covers on but no other protective clothing.

"I know, but we had no idea what we were going to find," Jordan said. "We didn't touch anything."

"I should hope not." Steve looked at the desk and then turned to examine the other hardware. He whistled through his teeth as he bent to examine the equipment. "Bloody hell," he muttered, "this guy meant business."

"I guess you know what it all is?"

"Yes, and this is quite a set-up." He pointed at the shelving. "Routers and a NAS – oh sorry, a network-attached storage device, that's for making backups. See here this is your network switch, that routes everything around. I won't know until I have the chance to get into it all properly, but I'll bet there are two internet lines here and one of them will be used anonymously."

"Not really sure how that works." Jordan was already out of his depth, but he still needed the information.

"He'd be running his own VPN software for end-to-end encryption to access the Tor network. You've heard of that?"

"I think so. Something about onions."

Even behind the mask Jordan could make out Steve's grin.

"The Onion Router. Loads of layers, you see, like – well, like an onion. So, this effectively hides where the traffic comes from by feeding through multiple other computers. I don't reckon we'll be able to do much with these if they are encrypted at hard drive level, even the password will require a 2-factor authentication device."

"Sorry, no clue what you mean," said Jordan.

"You know, something like a YubiKey."

"You be what?"

"Ha, well never mind. What it means effectively is that we're not getting into this. He might have used one of the machines on an unencrypted connection and that'll give us something, but the rest of this stuff, well… sorry."

"But I thought you could find anything, that's what I've always heard, even if the hard drive is damaged."

"Yes, on an ordinary, everyday set-up, and we can get logs from tech companies to help, but I don't reckon that's what we're talking about here. I have to say, boss, don't hold your breath waiting for much information from this lot. We'll give it a go, of course, but…" He shook his head.

"Okay, well do what you can, eh? Thanks, Steve."

Jordan turned and walked, slump-shouldered, back to the car. He had thought, when he saw the computer room, they'd have all the evidence they needed, but apart from the fact that such a set-up pointed to evil-doing, it wouldn't be any use as proof from a legal standpoint if they couldn't access what was hidden beneath the layers of protection.

Maybe they could approach it from the other angle. Maybe they could ask the public protection unit to search for Maisie on the stuff they were viewing, and he would talk to David Griffiths. He had mentioned a charity that searched for videos of abuse. If Brian Beetham had filmed Maisie and possibly Jean, then he'd done it for a reason and chances were that it was out there in the foulness of the dark web.

Chapter 60

It was good to feel the buzz in the incident room. Jordan had called Stella to update her, but her phone had gone to voicemail. If she was so ill that she couldn't even answer her phone, there was no point bothering her.

It took little to no time before they had the registration number for Brian Beetham's van and Jordan felt his pulse rate rise as he waited to hear that the bloke had been spotted. He was ready to go, but as the time went on and there was no word, he paced the room willing his phone to ring. A couple of hours went by and there was nothing.

"Okay. He's not on the road, is he?" Jordan said to John Grice. "Is there anything from the digital technical bods?"

Grice called the lab. They had impounded the equipment and were in the process of moving it to their workshop. They wouldn't even begin to access the data without safety checks and even then, it would be a long job to examine the drives without risking compromising anything on there. This was always assuming they could break through the heavy-duty protection.

Grice paused for a minute and then he let a grin stretch his lips. "The SOCO team have played a blinder though, boss…" He paused and wiggled his eyebrows.

"Christ, John, you're like one of those comperes on the reality shows, just get on with it."

The scene of crime team had been unable to search the computer room because the technical department were taking it apart. They had done their usual job in the living rooms and kitchen and found very little and no sign of violence. Hairs and other forensic samples would be sent away for analysis, but there was no blood or indication that anyone had been kept captive. The garage had held nothing apart from a couple of empty boxes and some half-empty paint tins.

In the bedroom they had searched the built-in furniture which was almost empty. Grice referred to his notes.

"They said there were bits and pieces of clothing but not as much as you would expect. In the bathroom they found the usual stuff until they took the cover off the front of the bath – and…"

"And…" Jordan knew he was being played with and grinned. "Come on – and…"

Grice pulled out a chair from the desk next to the one that Jordan was using and dragged it close.

"They found a box. Wrapped in plastic and stuffed under the bath. They have it back in the lab and it's taken them a while to open it with all the precautions and that. But inside there are DVDs."

"DVDs."

"Yes, old-fashioned of course, but professional-looking, with proper boxes and printed labels. The labels show just dates and a couple of initials."

Jordan swallowed hard. "Okay, so you've been leading up to this. What was on them – I'm assuming it's not Shirley Bassey in concert?"

"It is not. They are copying one and sending the content to your machine. Just yours for now because they have warned that it's difficult viewing."

Jordan picked up his laptop and with a 'come with me' gesture to John Grice, he walked along the corridor to an unused office.

They sat side by side in front of a dusty desk and watched young Maisie, tethered, tortured, and filmed.

When the footage ended neither of them spoke for some time.

"Okay," Grice said, finally, "I've spoken briefly to Steve the geek who is up to his armpits in Beetham's equipment. He says that the only way he can explain this is that he was catering to people who didn't have the complicated set-up he did and was simply selling them discs. A bit like selling dirty postcards or porn magazines. Anyway, he must have forgotten they were there or, more likely, hasn't had a chance to go back and get them before we invaded his space."

"I don't think there is any need to show this to the rest of the team, we'll leave her a bit of dignity, such as it is."

"She escaped though, didn't she?"

"She must have done. God knows how, tethered like that, but she can't have been thrown into the canal while she was still alive, that doesn't make sense. It's not a way to get rid of a body. Not unless he's totally stupid. No, the poor thing must have made a run for it."

They knew they would need to watch the film again because they had to take more from it than horror and disgust.

"We need to find him and that place," Jordan said as he closed his laptop. "We're going to start at the community centre. We know he's been there recently and it's as good a place as any to kick off."

As they swung into the incident room to collect coats he called out, "Kath, keep me completely up to date. Anything at all I need to know straight away."

* * *

The school attached to the centre was closed for the day. There were classes scheduled for later in the evening but nothing was happening at all in the meeting hall when they arrived. The door was unlocked, presumably for setting up classrooms or whatever. The place had an abandoned feel. They called out as they walked through and were met with silence.

"Caretakers and cleaners usually have a storeroom or a workroom or something, don't they?" Jordan said. "I'm going out into the yard where the image showed his van. You have a mooch around here, buzz me if you find anything."

The lean-to at the end of the building was hidden from the road and the car park. It was a flat-roofed concrete construction with a small window in the side wall and double metal doors locked and chained. Jordan rattled the chain, but it was hefty and sound. He had choices. There might be a key somewhere, probably with the manager of the place, though the last news of him was that he was ill in hospital. There could be one in the school which was closed. Maybe somewhere in one of the rooms, but no idea which one or how they were kept. They could spend ages searching and maybe there were none there at all. He looked around. Against the wall were some lumps of wood and a couple of what appeared to be broken railings.

Well, it would be silly not to.

He hefted one of the railings – it might work. It took a couple of tries. He wasn't after all experienced at breaking and entering. A chain is only as strong as the weakest link, and it was that which gave way. The chain, still attached to the padlock, shuttered to the floor with a clatter.

The door swung outwards, opening onto a short corridor. Jordan switched on the light. A small cupboard was neatly stacked with the expected chemicals, mop heads, and buckets. The smell was just as he remembered from his own school days, something soapy backed with a sharp note which might have been from any one of the cans and bottles. Opposite was another door, locked, and then another door down the short hallway. This was also locked. There seemed to be an unreasonable amount of security but then there were the chemicals and children could conceivably come this way.

Jordan rattled the door handle and shook his head at the futile gesture. He stepped back a couple of paces and charged it with his shoulder to no avail. He called out, "Jean, Jean Barker, police. Are you in there?"

It wasn't a great surprise that there was no response, but he had to acknowledge a moment of disappointment. It would have been too good to be true. He still wanted access.

"You okay, boss?" John Grice had joined him quietly. "Still nobody in the hall and nothing that seems out of the ordinary. What's this?"

"Dunno. I'd like to get in but it's pretty sturdy. I suppose we'll have to find the key or call a locksmith and that means a warrant. I could justify an entry because I do believe it's possible Jean is in here. Unlikely, I admit, but…" He shrugged.

"Mind out the way then," Grice said.

He spent a moment looking at the hinges and knocked on the body of the door. He nodded, raised his right leg, and touched his foot to just below the handle. Two sharp breaths and a moment with his eyes closed were followed by a powerful kick with the flat of his foot against the door. It didn't move but they heard a crack.

"Bloody hell. Where did you learn to do that?"

"Kickboxing. They don't exactly teach you how to kick down doors, but I guess you could call it a spin-off. Anyway, it's not open yet, give me some room."

Two more sharp kicks and the door swung back forcefully and bounced against the wall. It was dark in the room and the foul stench was overwhelming.

"Jesus, that's ripe," Grice said.

Jordan had taken out his phone and switched on the light. He had smelled a dead body before, many of them had, but he didn't believe that was what they had found.

He held out an arm to prevent John Grice stepping any further into the space.

In the corner, by the harsh brightness of his torch, they saw the bucket, a few crumpled pieces of paper and a ring screwed into the wall. The floor beside the ring marked with dark stains. Jordan turned to shine the light onto the opposite wall. High in the corner they could make out a small bracket, and a hole drilled into the wall to allow a cable through. Other corners had similar marks but no equipment.

"Okay. We need to secure this scene. I'll contact the station, we need a crime scene manager, scene of crime technicians – the whole nine yards. Now. All-ports alert. If Beetham knows we're on to him he'll make a run for it."

Chapter 61

When the call came from the digital department it held no surprise. Jordan had been prepared but it was still a huge disappointment to know that they couldn't access the hidden files.

"Nobody could, boss," Steve said. "Honest, even the FBI, MI5, there is a limit to what you can do, and this is a bloody well protected set-up. He knew what he was doing, this bloke. Except of course for the parcel in the bathroom which is still boggling my mind."

In some ways it didn't matter now but they would continue to try.

At the community centre it didn't take long for the whole circus to arrive followed by the head of the school who had taken on temporary responsibility for the place.

Jordan took her into one of the quiet rooms. He kept the more gruesome details to himself. After giving her a brief outline of the case, he simply told her that she would have to close the centre until further notice, and he couldn't really say for how long.

A technician came to whisper in Jordan's ear that the other locked room contained shelving and banks of sockets and they believed it had been used for electronic equipment.

"I was at the bloke's flat, boss, and this looks to me like a minor version of that studio. Empty now, unfortunately."

Jordan turned back to the head teacher. "We need to find the caretaker as a matter of urgency. What do you know about him?"

He had worked in both the school and community hall for longer than the headmistress had been around. She knew very little about him except that he was good at his job and never minded working extra if they had parents' evenings and suchlike.

"He was pretty much left to his own devices. As long as the work was done, that's all we were bothered about. I can't believe he's been keeping someone locked in his workshop. You must be wrong. I'm sure there'll be an explanation. Maybe it was a homeless person, and he was just giving them somewhere safe during the pandemic."

Jordan didn't bother to disabuse her of the idea. She would hear the full facts in time anyway. He asked if they had a picture of Beetham, a staff photograph or anything like that, and she promised to have a look.

"He's not a member of the teaching staff so we wouldn't have him on the 'get to know us' board. I might be able to find something though."

There was very little more he could do. They made their way back to the station where news of the films and DVDs had spread in the way such things always did.

"The most important thing now is to find out everything we can about this person," Jordan said. "Jean Barker wasn't at his flat and she wasn't in his workshop.

I'm sure that they'll find evidence of Maisie and probably Jean, DNA if we're lucky. But where is he now? Where is she? He has another place. Send me everything you've got, Kath. Can you make sure the board is updated? Then you can bugger off home. You've put in a good shift, and we've made brilliant progress. Everyone who can, please come in tomorrow."

Chapter 62

"You staying on, boss?" Grice asked.

"I am. I've managed to get a spot on the local news," Jordan said. "We've been provided with a picture of Beetham. It's old, taken from a school open day photograph and it's not the best quality, but it's better than nothing. I just want to make it impossible for him to move around."

"It doesn't look as though he has tried to leave the country, unless he did a bunk before we got on to him."

"That's a good point. Before we go, can you make sure the image is circulated to everyone who needs to see it? He hasn't got a passport as far as we know, but with his computer skills and dark web contacts I wouldn't be surprised if he managed to get a dodgy one."

"But would he just leave Mrs Barker do you reckon?"

"Yeah, I think so if she became too hot to handle. Or of course if she was no longer any use to him." He didn't need to spell out what the reason for that would be.

Jordan opened the files on his computer, Beetham's life story such as it was. He scrolled through the information. After an hour he glanced up to see John Grice standing by the window sipping at a cup of coffee that must have been stewed and bitter.

"Fancy a bevy, John?"

"Yeah, great. Just the one."

* * *

They had both known when they went to the pub that they would talk about the case, but it didn't matter. Sometimes throwing around ideas away from the high-pressure surroundings of the incident room paid dividends.

"You heard from the DS, boss?"

"I tried to call her but no answer."

"Are you worried about her?"

"Well, I'll be glad to see her back, but I wouldn't say I'm worried exactly."

"Oh right. I just thought…"

"Thought what?"

"Well, you're close, aren't you? You've worked together before, in Kirkby."

"We're mates, John. Nothing more than friends and colleagues, and actually, if you know who it is that's saying it's more than that I'd appreciate you putting them right. Okay?"

Grice held up his hands in submission.

There was a minute of silence and then the case gave them a way out of the awkwardness.

There had been nothing to note in the bank accounts. Beetham had a small amount in savings, but only the equivalent of about a month's salary. There were no unexplained payments either in or out. It was all unremarkable.

Grice took a big drink of his lager and wiped his mouth.

"I was talking to Steve after we got back this affy. As he thought, there were two internet lines. One of them wasn't anonymous and he had a technician looking at that. They couldn't find Beetham much on social media. No Facebook. His Twitter account hadn't been very active for a few years. The odd comment now and then with old mates from college. Apart from that it just seems everything he did was off-grid. He reckons the reason we can't find any real money is because it's all in cryptocurrency."

"I've never quite got my head around that stuff. I know it makes life more difficult for us, doesn't it? Another way to hide ill-gotten gains."

"Yes, Steve the geek had my head spinning again. Can you imagine what's it's like inside his brain? Jesus, he's not like the rest of us, I swear. Anyway, I knew about Bitcoin of course, but he was going on about hardware wallets, Ledger Nano something and Monero which is what hackers use. We'd never find it. If he can't, we don't stand a chance."

"Thing is though, if he had a heap of money, even if it was cryptocurrency, what does he do with it? He's not a young man saving for his future, and surely he'd want to benefit from it now. Would he not buy things?"

"I guess. But what? Okay, computer equipment, but we've seen all that."

"I wonder if we have. That flat was pretty spartan, wasn't it? Pretty grim, really, and no sign that he was actually living there properly," Jordan said.

"Somewhere else, maybe another house. Is that what you're thinking? Or maybe he's got a boat or a giant camper van."

"God, I hope not. He'll be in the wind if that's the case. No, I was thinking maybe somewhere isolated. He probably could only use the room at the community centre during the lockdown. The school was effectively closed, just a few kids and a couple of teachers and the centre was shut up totally. I wonder if he just made use of that because he could and there's somewhere else, somewhere better suited to what he was up to. Maybe we've just been really lucky finding that room. It's all evidence for the CPS that points at him and no-one else."

"What about the flat though?" Grice said.

"I don't know. Maybe it was just another place to use. Could be that he owns it, but I don't think for a minute he was living there full time."

They sat for a while in quiet, sipping at the warming beer until they agreed to start again the next morning.

"Sorry about earlier, boss," Grice said. "You know, about the Stella thing."

"It's okay. I know there've been rumours but it's just ridiculous. You'd think people had better things to talk about."

"Well anyway, I apologise."

"It's fine. Let's just concentrate on finding this bastard."

Chapter 63

The next morning Jordan crept around the kitchen careful not to rattle cups and clatter cutlery. It was Saturday and Penny deserved a bit of a lie-in before Harry woke her. But as he stared out at the dark garden and drank his coffee, he felt his wife's arms wrap around his waist. He turned and bent to kiss her.

"Didn't hear you come in last night," she said.

He knew it wasn't a complaint and when he told her how late he had been she simply nodded.

"There's no good news, is there?"

He shook his head. He could tell her about their findings, but it wouldn't help, and he didn't want to spoil her day with dark images.

"Working on it as much as I can. Might be another late one."

"Take care, love."

"Always."

With that he grabbed his jacket and bag and then drove through the quiet Crosby streets and out towards Aintree.

* * *

John Grice was already at his desk. "This bloke had a pretty rotten start in life by the look of things. Foster care until he was old enough to be ejected from the system. He did well to finish a college degree. I wonder what went wrong after that."

"I really hope that we have the chance to ask him," Jordan said.

Beetham had gone into care at age eight when the family unit had broken down. At age sixteen he should have transitioned into adult care but that didn't happen. He simply fell out of sight. The next thing they had was his record from John Moores University.

"He graduated with a two-one, which isn't bad," Grice said. "Then the next thing we have are his jobs here and there. Nothing using his degree."

"The university must have had an address for him while he was with them. I know it's a while ago, but it could be helpful. Get on to that, will you?"

Stella called later in the morning and, in spite of himself, when he saw her name on his screen Jordan took the phone into the corridor to answer.

"Still testing positive but I'm feeling more human. How's your Nana?"

"Getting better thanks."

"Anyway, what can I do to help?"

Jordan brought her up to date and sent her all the information she didn't already have.

"Do you want to see the film of Maisie? It's very grim."

"I should. Send it over. Poor thing. I suppose we are pretty clear now that her appointment was with Beetham."

When Jordan finished the call, he replayed the conversation, and he just couldn't see how Maisie would have gone to meet the caretaker. Why would she think that he could help her with her career? She had said that it was an unexpected contact, but she wouldn't expect Beetham to make her a model. So if it was him, he must have been acting as a go-between. If there was someone else, then that might explain the other location. Jordan felt a familiar buzz of excitement.

Chapter 64

The team were busy, mainly answering the responses to the item on the news and in the *Echo*.

Jordan poured fresh coffee into his insulated mug, left John Grice in charge, and drove himself to the parade of shops with Beetham's flat upstairs.

There was a constable on the door being taunted by a group of children running back and forth along the narrow walkway, making grunting noises and comments about roast pork. Old taunts but still doing the rounds. As Jordan approached, they switched to monkey squeals. He'd seen it and worse many times before, both in London and since he'd come to Merseyside. Maybe by the time Harry was grown-up it would stop happening. He hoped so. He didn't want his boy to put up with everything he and his brothers had gone through. But he could do nothing about it and there was more to think about right now.

"Anything happening, Constable?" he asked. "Apart from the local idiots."

He took a short report of nosy neighbours and a couple of reporters from Radio Merseyside and then told the uniformed officer to take a break.

"I'm going inside to have a look round and see if I can get a feel for this bloke. Should be about an hour so don't rush back."

He ducked under the crime scene tape.

The flat had been bleak on his first visit but now, covered with the residue from fingerprint powder and the fitted cupboard doors hanging open, it looked derelict. The kitchen was empty apart from the fridge which someone had switched off.

In the bathroom the plastic front of the bath was leaning against the wall. Underneath, the cavity was dirty and dusty and filled with spiderwebs. There was still an evidence tent showing where the little package had been found.

The computer room was empty of equipment. He stood in front of the desk. The swivel chair was in the lab, but he was certain anything of note had already been photographed and swabbed and dusted. He was quiet for a while considering the things that might have happened in this small space and the vile things that had been recorded and transmitted to the twisted individuals who viewed such stuff.

From outside there was the low rumble of cars on the road and the occasional screech from a child. A dog barked in the distance. He had hoped that coming here would maybe help him imagine the life of Brian Beetham and maybe give him some idea of where the man could have gone but there was nothing of him. He had used this place as a studio and nothing more. Now they had to go back to square one with the search for his home.

The click of the front knob brought all his senses to high alert. Was this just the bobby coming back to stand guard or someone else? The hairs on his arms raised and his nerve endings tingling, Jordan moved to behind the door, peering through the gap into the hallway beyond.

Chapter 65

He remembered meeting Brian Beetham when they had gone to the yoga class before they had any idea just what he was about. He still appeared ordinary, perhaps a little bigger than Jordan remembered. Out of his overalls and without his mop and bucket he looked younger and fitter. Standing straight-backed with none of the stooped posture of someone for whom life was less than fun, he was more imposing.

He pulled the door closed behind him, holding a hand against the wood so that it made little more than a quiet click as the latch engaged.

He looked around the room and frowned at what he saw. The scene of crime technicians had moved furniture and Beetham pushed the flimsy coffee table out of his way with a foot. Jordan could show himself now, arrest this individual and the case would be over. He took a breath, readied himself. He expected that there would be a struggle, but he had the advantage of surprise and felt well able to take the other man even in this new guise.

He gripped the door handle and watched as Beetham walked towards the kitchen. He should wait until he was well into the flat so that it would make it harder for him to run, and if he waited until his back was turned, all the better.

The heavy knock on the door took him by surprise. Beetham stopped for a second and then turned to head back across the living room to peer out of the window. Jordan waited in the quiet bathroom.

The man at the door was younger and better-dressed than Beetham, who was casual in jeans and a hoody top.

The smart suit looked out of place in such grubby, decrepit surroundings.

"Come in, quick," Beetham said.

The door was pushed closed as the newcomer looked around, his nose wrinkling at the condition of the flat.

"They did a number on this place then?" The accent wasn't Liverpudlian. There was a faint regional burr, possibly southern, Home Counties.

"Bloody filth. My mam would have been fit to burn. All she had was this place and even that didn't bring her any luck. I'm gonna get rid now. It was never really my home anyway," Beetham said.

"They got all the equipment?"

"I haven't seen yet. I've only just come. You didn't move that tape, did you? Don't want anyone to know I'm in here."

Jordan slid his hand into his pocket and pulled out the phone. First he turned the device to silent, and then switched on the recording app.

"Might as well see the damage," Beetham said, as he led the other man towards the hallway on the way to the box room. "Bloody hell. When I saw that on the telly and in the *Echo* I knew they'd be round here before long. Ha, I would have liked to have seen their faces. Bet that was a surprise for them. Still, it's not funny, looks like they've taken all my stuff. Don't worry, Rich. They won't be able to get nothing off of it. The protection is sound. Not even bloody Zuckerberg could do it."

"Well, that's not saying much, anyway. But good. So we need to collect the other stuff and then it's time to move on. We've done well here but it's time to leave."

"It's all that bloody young bird's fault. There would have been no need for any of this if it hadn't been for her."

"You shouldn't have let her get away. I have to tell you, the boss isn't happy about that. If anything comes back to him, you'll be very sorry."

"Don't be getting at me," Beetham said, "I was just trying to make some good films. I was trying to liven things up, wasn't I? I thought it'd got boring. Could have been better viewing if she was crawling around with no chain. You know, like a mad tiger in the zoo or something. I didn't think she had enough left in her to run. Anyway listen, you tell the boss it turned out alright. I'll bet the filth reckon she just drowned. Silly cow jumping the bridge. All day I'd been looking for her and then she does that at the last minute. You were no bloody help neither when you did eventually turn up."

"But why the other woman? That's really effed things up. Why didn't you just leave it for a while? Let things settle."

"She asked for it, she annoyed me. Bloody arrogant cow, pathetic old boot."

"You knew her? Please tell me you didn't know her."

"Nah, I didn't know her, know her, but she was always at that yoga class poncing about like Lady Muck. Would I like a biscuit, did I want help cleaning up? I used to look at her and think about what she'd look like if I got my hands on her. Then the day that other bitch ran, I saw her. Early, before you came, while I was out looking on the road and she gave me the finger just because I splashed her bloody trousers. She didn't know it was me, though. It's soundo."

"It was still a stupid move. Especially if anybody at the centre can connect you."

"Course they bloody can't. I've told you. I used to ignore the snotty old bag."

"Okay I've seen enough here. Let's collect the stuff from the bathroom and then get out of here," Rich said.

"What about my money?"

"You'll be lucky after this cock-up."

"Right. I'm off then," Beetham said. "Going to keep out of the way for a bit. I'll come back when the fuss has died down. We alright to set up somewhere else? I like the place I'm at now, but I reckon I'll have to go. Clear it out, like, and then that's me gone."

"I'll speak to the boss."

Jordan knew it was time to move. What were the chances that he would be able to arrest both men and restrain them, on his own, and hold them until backup came?"

There was only one way to find out.

Chapter 66

It was a momentary decision. Jordan had tensed behind the door and prepared for violence. They were coming now, out of the box room towards his hiding place in the bathroom. He had enough recorded on his phone to start to build a case.

If he tried to arrest these men now it was conceivable that he wouldn't be able to manage on his own. He knew that. He had no illusions about his abilities. He was fit, but he was no superhero. He could be hurt and become useless to a team already depleted by illness.

Further, if one of them escaped, what did that mean for Jean Barker? Even if he did manage to overpower two tough-looking men, any chance they had of finding Jean would be reduced. News of their arrest would soon reach whoever else was involved. It was useless to believe otherwise. It was impossible to know what others might do to Jean if they had to leave in a hurry and thought they might be named by the two lower-echelon thugs who had been caught.

Jordan took out his mobile phone and made sure the location tracking was activated. Just in case.

He sidled rapidly around the bathroom door frame and into the second bedroom. He didn't dare to push the door in case the movement was seen, so he pressed tight against the wall, hardly breathing. He waited for the explosion of anger when Beetham and his mate found the empty space under the bath.

The yell was loud and followed quickly by the crash of the plastic bath front as someone kicked out in fury.

Scuffling and scraping evidenced a frantic search that both men probably realised was useless.

The shouted conversation that followed was a tumble of foul language, recrimination, and name-calling. It was followed by a brief silence broken by a voice containing a note of panic.

"Right, that's it, we have to move. Now, today, in the next couple of hours. Everything has to be cleared and we have to be gone. Those discs can be accessed by anyone. Once they have those they'll find where they were taken. You'll be sorry about this. This is a big mistake. Greed has got you here and you'll be sorry."

Jordan thought it was the man called Rich who was speaking.

There were more angry words, and then the two men stamped across the bare boards. Jordan heard the door wrench open as they left, slamming it behind them.

He was at the window in seconds and recording while they scurried along the concrete walkway. As they reached the stairs he was through the door, near enough to see but keeping out of sight. The kids who had been there earlier were approaching across the shopping square. He had to be gone before they saw him and maybe started again with the name-calling and harassment. He was six steps from the bottom and vaulted sideways over the wall onto the hard asphalt below. He rolled as he landed and although he was covered in damp, dirty litter and something wet had stained the leg of his trousers, he wasn't hurt.

Beetham and his companion were heading for the parking area at the rear of the shopping centre. Jordan ran on as he speed-dialled John Grice.

He gave him a breathless and truncated account of events, and once he was near enough, the registration number of the car now being driven out of the car park by the man called Rich.

"I'm going to follow Beetham, he's in the white van. I reckon he'll go to where he has Jean Barker. John, you know what to do."

Chapter 67

The man called Rich was long gone. Driving a Jaguar F-Pace Sport that turned heads, he didn't hang around to enjoy the admiration. He took the roundabout at speed and disappeared.

Beetham, in his more modest vehicle, threaded out of the parking area, and joined the line of early Saturday evening traffic. As far as Jordan was aware, the man had no idea what car he drove, and apparently didn't have any reason to believe he was being followed. He didn't know Jordan had heard the discussion in the flat.

Tucking the VW Golf into the line of traffic just two cars back from the white van, Jordan slid his phone onto the holder on the dash and waited for the Bluetooth to connect.

They turned out of Browns Lane over the canal and into Copy Lane. When they joined Dunnings Bridge Road they headed north. Jordan called John Grice.

"Have you mobilised backup? I don't want to pick up the other bloke – Rich something – until we have Mrs Barker safe, so make sure everyone knows he is only to be followed. For now I need to know where Beetham is headed without alerting him. This is possibly our only hope of finding Jean. We can't cock this up."

He contacted the communications room and the officer assigned to the pursuit.

"I need air support, but I need them to hang back unless I call them in. This is not a high-speed pursuit. He doesn't know I'm following him. We're heading for Switch Island. I need unmarked cars on the M57, the M58, the A59 and the A578. As soon as I know which way we're headed, I'll let you know. I need this to stay low key."

"Okay. Keep me informed, sir. You are pursuit commander."

As far as he was concerned it wasn't a pursuit. Jordan didn't want it to become a pursuit because he knew that would probably mean failure. No matter, the finer points could be discussed later and at least this way he was in charge and could take whatever action he needed to.

The Switch Island lights were changing as they approached. If Beetham went through on amber, it would be over unless Jordan jumped the lights from two cars behind. That wasn't going to happen. The white van was positioned in the lane for the A59. If he was driving correctly then that would mean he wasn't heading for the motorway. On the one hand this meant his speed was restricted, but the Saturday evening traffic heading for Ormskirk and Southport on the narrower roads would make following the nondescript vehicle more difficult. There were three other white vans in this queue alone.

The lights flicked to red. At first it seemed that Beetham may speed through but a motorbike from the M57 had screeched up the slip road and crossed the junction. The white van shuddered to a halt, front wheels over the stop line. Around him traffic slowed, and someone sounded an angry horn.

Jordan contacted the control room and asked for an update. An unmarked car was on the way but wasn't near enough yet to be of much help.

"I've got a marked car in Maghull. He's at Central Square."

"Okay, but I don't want this bloke alerted. I just need more eyes on him. Is there any news of the air support?"

"Hawarden are mobilising, but they had nothing immediately available. I'll keep you updated."

There was nothing more he could do. If he had simply wanted to arrest Beetham this would have been easy. The marked car from Maghull could have joined the party and between them they would have forced the van to stop. Once they had reached the relatively open area approaching Aughton, they could even have used the spike strip. They could take the bloke in now. But that wouldn't help Jean.

For now he would stay behind him, fingers crossed and asking Nana Gloria's god for a bit of help.

Chapter 68

Jordan didn't know the area around Ormskirk well, but he knew that the little town could clog up with traffic. From what he remembered, Saturday was market day and the roads were even busier than normal. He had been this way before. It was rural, and once away from the town it was a patchwork of fields, farms, riding schools, kennels, and catteries. He contacted John Grice.

"Go through Beetham's employment records. See if he worked anywhere round Burscough, Ormskirk, that sort of area."

The marked car from Maghull was in the outside lane. As they passed, the officer in the passenger seat turned and nodded at Jordan. So they knew which car was his. They pulled ahead of the line of traffic and back into the inside lane a couple of vehicles in front of Beetham. It was clever work because they were at the speed limit, and it was unlikely that anyone would break the law to overtake the police. The white van was effectively trapped between Jordan and the patrol car but had no idea of his situation. Jordan grinned. He'd buy that driver a pint when this was over. The white van was three cars ahead of him now and he couldn't see the indicator lights.

The turn was sudden and unexpected. It was luck on the part of Beetham, but the marked car was involved in the complicated junction into Moss Delph Lane, slowing to see which way they should go and dealing with turning traffic joining the main road.

Jordan flashed his headlights as he took the corner into the B5195, a two-lane highway winding out into the countryside, but had no way of knowing whether or not the support officers had seen him go. He was on his own again.

He updated the control room. "I've lost the other car, any news on air support?"

"We're doing all we can, should be with you in a few minutes now. They've been told the situation."

Beetham increased his speed. He most likely assumed there was no traffic monitoring away from the main roads and was probably correct.

Hidden pursuit was more difficult now. There were no other cars to hide behind. Although it was not as straight as the major road, it was more open than Jordan would have liked. He hung back as far as he dared but didn't know the route or direction Beetham would take. By the time he reached the unexpected mini-roundabout at the junction of Formby Lane, he had lost sight of the van. He went around the junction twice and then pulled in with two wheels on the narrow pavement, thumped a hand on the steering wheel and let loose a string of expletives.

Chapter 69

"What do you want to do, sir?" the woman in the control room asked. "Do you want the air support withdrawn?"

Now it wasn't so good being pursuit commander. With moments to decide, Jordan's mind was racing. In the end he still wanted to protect Jean Barker. If the helicopter with its eye in the sky and the rattle of rotor blades were to circle over the fields near Aughton there was no way Beetham would ignore it.

"Stand them down for now. Any news of the patrol car or my unmarked backup?"

"The patrol car should be with you soon; other cars are on the way."

He could sit and wait, or he could move now, trawl around the roads, which were almost completely dark, and hope that he might spot the van. Trouble was he had no idea what Beetham's plan had been driving away from the main road. It could have been a shortcut to somewhere else entirely and he was now en route to Southport, Morecambe, or even the Lakes.

John Grice rang through. "I'm coming out there to help, boss. I'm in the car now with Kath. In the meantime you should know that Beetham worked at a school out that way six years ago."

"Do you have any details?"

"He was caretaker. Left in the middle of a term which was odd. I've got a call in to the ex-headteacher who worked with him, but no response yet."

"Where was the school?"

"Aughton. A church school."

"Okay, so he hasn't headed there, he's gone the other way. I'm going to continue driving round but this is a total cock-up and it's all my fault. I should have grabbed him while I had the chance."

There was no answer from the other man.

When Stella's name popped up on the phone screen he almost didn't answer. He had no time right now to give her sympathy and updates but, in the end, it felt wrong to ignore his mate.

"I've been monitoring what's going on via the airwaves set and Kath on the phone, Jordan. You're out towards Ormskirk? I've been going through this stuff on Beetham. He was driving that van when he got done for having a headlight out and two bald tyres."

"Not that helpful right now, Stella, he's given me the slip so I can't see his tyres."

"Oh, shut up. The important thing is the address he gave at the time. He was living in a house out there. It might be worth having a look."

"Can you send me the coordinates?"

"Already done it. I had a look on Google Earth. It's a bit of a remote place. I can't make out what it really is now, but it used to be a riding stable years ago. Oh by the way, I've tested negative and I'm in the car on the way out to join you. No way you're winding this up on your own."

Chapter 70

There were patrol cars converging from every direction. Normally this would be brilliant, unexpected on a Saturday night with officers deployed elsewhere. Jordan didn't want them. Okay the switched-on driver from Northway had done the best he could but there wasn't time to fill him in on the details of the case. Marked cars would alert Beetham to the fact that they were following him, and blues and twos were the last thing they needed right now.

Stella and John Grice could be useful, but they weren't here, and he needed to find Jean Barker immediately. The conversation in the flat hadn't given him any idea of her condition but it couldn't be good. He didn't imagine Beetham and his thuggish mates would be sending her home or even taking her anywhere with them. She was of no further use. Expendable.

There was so little time.

He entered the coordinates for the old house that had possibly been Beetham's home and followed the gentle voice of Google directions.

It wasn't far. He turned at the next junction, a sharp left just a few metres along the lane and there it was. '*You have arrived at your destination.*'

He didn't slow but drove past the dilapidated house and barns. An estate agents' board had been taken down and laid along the side of the fence. There was a five-bar gate half open across the weedy entrance.

Jordan parked his car near a partly constructed bungalow. Metal barriers had been dragged across the entrance and there was no sign of life. There was a security light mounted on a post and as he climbed out of his car it flicked on, bathing the whole area in brilliant white. Not ideal but it had happened, move on.

He crossed the road and jogged back towards the house. There were several old buildings, all in the same poor state. The house was in darkness. Jordan clambered into the field behind the barns and staggered across the ridges and furrows. He should have put his boots on. They were in the car for just this scenario. It didn't matter much now. Move on. The white van was tucked into a corner of the yard, invisible from the road. The rear doors were open.

He couldn't use his torch.

There was a wire fence between him and the yard. He reached out gingerly. It may be electrified and though he knew the shock would be mild, he didn't want it. There was no jolt. He clambered carefully over and landed with a grating crunch on the damp gravel.

He backed into the deeper shadows and took a moment to get his bearings. The phone in his pocket vibrated. He dragged it out and fired off a text to Stella. He told her his location and asked her to park at the junction with Formby Lane and keep her eyes peeled for the van in case he made a sudden run for it.

"A patrol car might be with you soon. Once it arrives move on down the road. Park beyond the house. You'll see my car."

The back door of the house swung open and the narrow beam of Beetham's torch picked out the puddles and piles of rubbish as he strode across the small distance to throw a suitcase into the back of the van. He went back inside leaving the rear doors open.

A minute passed. Jordan could storm in now and take him. This had to be where Jean was being kept, surely. He tensed for the sprint across the yard. The door opened again. This time there were three metal suitcases that Beetham handled with care. It was chilling to think that it was probably the equipment used to make the filthy videos they had seen.

Beetham went back a second time. He left the van doors open and the house door ajar.

Jordan crossed the yard and slid in through the back door. It smelled damp and dirty. Though there were no animals around, as far as he could see, but there was the stench of piles of abandoned manure in a dump near the sheds. There was furniture, but it was impossible to see the condition of it. The boards beneath his feet were bare, somewhere a tap dripped.

He heard the creak of the floor above him.

The staircase was narrow and dark. He placed his feet on the outsides of the steps, testing as he went, but the old, warped wood gave him away creaking and groaning as he moved.

A door above was flung open.

"Rich, is that you? You shouldn't have come here. I'm clearing out. Bugger off, I'll meet you at my place."

As he yelled out Beetham crossed the narrow landing to shine his light down onto the stairs. He was struggling with another instrument case, this one bigger than the other two. He gaped at Jordan, his face a picture of surprise but only for a moment. With a great yell he flung the heavy box downwards. Jordan raised his arms to protect himself, but the case glanced off the side of his head and bounced on down the steps. He tumbled back clawing out at the wooden banister. Beetham cleared the stairs two at a time and as he raced past, he took a moment to kick out at Jordan's head.

As the world turned dark, he heard the door slam back on its hinges and running footsteps crunching on the gravel outside.

Chapter 71

As the darkness receded Jordan became aware of the pain in his head. There was blood on his face, warm and sticky. He was nauseous and dizzy but he dragged himself upright with the aid of the wooden banister. The room spun and for a moment he had to close his eyes.

As the vertigo abated, he was already dragging the phone from his pocket and speed-dialling Stella.

"Are you following the van?"

"It's not come this way," she said. "I haven't seen it."

"He's gone. Bugger, he's gone the other way."

"I'll let John know he's on the main road. Are you okay, boss? Should I come down? I feel like a spare part here."

"Yeah, I'm fine but he's away. Get after him. You come straight down this road, past the house. I don't know exactly how long he's been gone. Not very long. You can catch him. Bring in the patrol car, he knows we're here now so we've nothing to lose."

"Is she there? Is Jean Barker in the house?"

"I don't know yet. I had a bit of a meeting with Beetham. I saw him taking out equipment, so I reckon she is. I'm going to go and look around. I'm a bit dizzy, probably shouldn't drive at the minute. When you see him, just follow him. He mentioned meeting at 'his place'. We need to find it. There will be evidence. I'll just look for Jean and get her sorted and then I'm after you. Keep me informed. I'll be there as soon as I can."

"Do you want me to call an ambulance?"

"Yeah, I reckon so. She'll need one. But I have to locate her first, this is a big rambling place. I'll let you know."

"Are you sure you're okay? Why are you dizzy?"

"It's okay, it's nothing. Just get moving."

The ground floor was filthy; the kitchen, such as it was, had no fitted units. There was an old gas stove, a Belfast sink, and a table in the centre of the room. There were a couple of packets of crisps and some cartons of juice. A crate of bottled water stood in the corner. The filthy window was covered by a net curtain, grey and limp.

In one corner was a wooden door. Jordan strode across the cracked lino and grabbed the knob. He had to stop for a minute while the room tipped and turned grey again. He wiped at the blood from his head which had slowed to a trickle.

"Jean, are you there? Mrs Barker, it's DI Carr, are you there?"

He stepped onto the plain wooden staircase and felt around for a light switch. When he flicked it, the small space was illuminated by a single bulb dangling on the end of a twisted cable. He could see at once that she wasn't there. Shelves around the walls held pans and oven trays. There was a row of jugs and piles of serving dishes. Everything was covered in a layer of dust. Nobody had been in there for a long time. He descended four steps which gave him a view of the whole cellar. She wasn't there. He turned and clambered into the kitchen and swung the door closed.

The living room was large and still had some furniture, a couple of easy chairs and a small sofa. There were bookshelves set into the chimney alcove with a couple of magazines flung onto the top of a cupboard.

She wasn't there.

He intended to jog up the stairs but immediately he picked up speed his head spun again. He had to lean against the wall until he was steady. There were four bedrooms, one bathroom, which was surprisingly clean, and one toilet which wasn't.

She wasn't there.

He had been in every room and there was no sign of her. He needed help now to search the outbuildings.

"Stella, what's happening?"

"In pursuit, boss. Heading towards Southport. John picked him up going through Ormskirk. He must have known a back way. What do you want us to do? Is she okay? Have you got her?"

"I haven't found her. Don't pick him up. I repeat, don't stop him. Jean Barker isn't in the house. I don't want him stopped until we have her. If she's not here she could be at what he described as 'his place'."

"Understood."

Jordan went out into the yard. It had started to drizzle cold rain and the coolness on his head helped to clear it. He glanced around. Where should he look? The video he had seen didn't look like the inside of a barn. The walls had been stone or brick, surely. He walked around the corner of the house. On the end was a single-storey lean-to, brick-built with a small window and a tiled roof. The door was solid wood with metal handles. There was a chain and padlock threaded through the metal.

He pulled on the chain, but it was heavy and sound. He banged on the boards.

"Jean Barker, DI Carr. You're okay. I'm going to get you out."

He knew he could be shouting into emptiness but if she was there, he needed her to know there was help coming.

In the biggest barn, the one near to the house, there were old farm implements. There was a hefty hammer, a pickaxe and a crowbar. He grabbed all three, and juggling with the load, strode back across the puddly ground.

It was hard-going. The chain wouldn't break, and it was difficult to use the hammer to smash the lock because it swung back and forth. He wasn't firing on all cylinders, and he knew he was making a dog's breakfast of it. He paused for a minute to take stock.

He jabbed at the gap between the two doors with the crowbar until the wood began to splinter. He pushed the flattened end of the steel rod into the gap and levered with all his reduced strength against the door. He felt it move but it didn't give. He pushed a little more and, resting his foot against the other side, he heaved on the bar. It didn't open but he felt it give a little more. He tried again. His head pounded and he wanted to lie down, but he persevered with the bar. He felt it give, and he felt it go, and the door cracked open enough that he could see inside.

He dragged his phone from his pocket and turned on the light. He shone it into the dim space.

"Jean, Jean Barker, are you there? It's okay. It's going to be okay."

She was there.

Chapter 72

Jordan used the airwaves set to let everyone know that he had found Jean Barker. There was a yell of joy from someone. He thought it was probably Stella. When it was finished, she came online.

"Shall I send the ambulance now?"

Jordan took a deep breath. "No, don't do that."

"Okay, boss. Are you taking her straight to Ormskirk Hospital? It will be quicker than waiting for the paramedics. If she's well enough."

"No, I'm not doing that." He waited for the message to sink in.

"Aw shit." This was from John Grice.

"No," from Stella.

"I'll get in touch with the station," Jordan said. "We need to mobilise a team. The usual stuff. Crime scene manager, SOCO, and the coroner. You guys carry on. I want that bastard. I want him more than I've ever wanted anything. I'll have to wait now and secure this scene. Soon as I can, I'll join you. Stella, don't you let him get away."

He had seen the huddle of Jean in the corner of the nasty little lean-to and called out to her a couple of time. He had slammed and hammered at the metal handles on the door until they had fallen taking the chain with them.

There had been no movement, no response at all to his calls and his noisy entrance. She hadn't shifted as he shone the light across to where she lay, and the way that her body was in a tight, small huddle told him all he needed to know. He couldn't touch her except to place two fingers on her neck to double-check what was already only too obvious. He closed her eyes. Not strictly in the rules but he couldn't leave her staring blindly at the wall where she had scraped at the dirt with her fingernails the name of her daughter, and a heart shape.

He turned away and sat on the cold flags. He had things to do, there was much to organise, but for now, just for this moment all he could do was fight to hold back the tears of anger, of sadness, and frustration. He had failed. He would catch the people responsible for this. He would make sure that no matter how big the gang, he would have a hand in rounding up each and every one of them.

* * *

He had no choice but to wait for the teams to arrive. Jordan tried to keep up to date with the pursuit. Tried to manage things from where he was sitting on the wet ground outside the little lean-to with Jean's body inside.

He was tired, dizzy, and sore and very, very sad.

As soon as the circus arrived, he handed over to the crime scene manager.

"Are you okay, mate? You look dead ropey to me. Are you sure you don't need a doctor? That's a horrible bash on your head and you look like a ghoul."

"I'm okay. Just look after Jean for me."

"I don't think you should be behind no wheel. Danger to yourself and others. That's just what I think."

"I'm fine. I took a bit of a knock, that's all."

He left them in the dark rain with the poor dead body to start their work. He knew someone would need to tell Mel Barker what had happened. He couldn't do it by phone, someone would have to go. It should be him. Right now though he needed to get to Southport and the rest of his squad. He had to be there when they took Brian Beetham into custody, and he had to be the one to question him.

The crime scene manager had been correct. Jordan knew he wasn't fit to drive. The dizziness came in waves, and he struggled to focus on the road signs. But he wasn't giving up. Not yet.

The road from Ormskirk took him out into the country. He drove as fast as he dared past the few pubs, farms and closed-up businesses.

Stella was on the phone constantly. She directed him around the outskirts of Southport through Ainsdale and on to Formby. They were now parked in a narrow road among the large, detached houses near the famous woods and the massive beach beyond the sand dunes.

"Bit posh this, boss. If this is his place, he didn't pay for it with the wages from being a caretaker," Stella said. "John Grice and Kath are here. Plus the patrol car and one of the unmarked vehicles. We're mob-handed but I wondered if we need armed officers. What do you reckon?"

"I reckon it would take a long time to arrange. Do you have any idea how many people are in there?"

"There are two cars. Beetham's white van and a Jaguar. I had a bit of a scout round. There's a garage but I reckon if there's a car in there it's been in for a while. There's stuff in front of the doors."

If there were just two of them then they should be able to arrest them with the officers already there. Unless they were armed. Then it was a whole different scenario. Another decision to take. Jordan tried to concentrate. He had other people depending on him now and there had already been too much death. He pulled to the side of the road and took a couple of deep breaths.

Chapter 73

He hated to do it, but he had to consider the rest of the team. The only sensible thing was to call for armed backup and storm the house. They would overwhelm the people inside and even if there were guns involved the odds would be on the side of the force. It would take time to organise, but it was the only way to do this safely.

"Hold where you are, Stella. I'm going to arrange for backup. Just observe for now."

He called David Griffiths. This should almost certainly now be under the control of the Serious and Organised division. There was no way Brian Beetham was working alone, not if he was making so much money. Perhaps it would turn out to be connected to the gang in Europe. That would be a feather in St Anne Street's cap and would solve the problems with the way it had been handled, depending on how they spun it. Anyway, apart from anything else Griffiths had clout and could move things along quickly.

There was no answer. He left a message for a call as soon as possible. This complicated matters. He rang Josh Martin and gave him a quick rundown of the situation.

Once he had handed over the organisation of backup, he drove on through Birkdale and pulled into the narrow road behind Stella's VW.

She climbed out, rushed to his car, and leaned down to peer in through his window.

"Bloody hell, Jordan. You shouldn't be here. Have you seen the side of your head?"

"Well no, that's a bit tricky from my angle."

"Yes, okay, ha ha. But still, you look horrible."

"Thanks. You don't look so good yourself."

"No, well – bloody virus. But seriously you should be in hospital. Or at least at home."

"Not happening. Not going anywhere until this scroat is under lock and key. You know I can't."

"How long before the ART get here?"

"I'm waiting for a call back."

John Grice jumped out of his car and jogged over to where they were.

"Kath's down the road, boss. Watching the front of the house. There's movement. He's loading up the van and the other bloke has turned his car around. I reckon they're having it on their toes any time now. How long before backup arrives?"

"Too long," Jordan said. "John, if they make a break for it follow the Jag, just pursuit for now. See where he goes. With luck he'll lead us to some of the others involved in this and anyway we'll have him. Stella, I'll come in your car if that's okay. We'll watch the van. We need to keep an eye on them and then feed back to the ART. I'll let Josh know what's going on."

As he spoke Kath ran along the road, she stayed close to the hedge. Waving her arms to let them know that at least one of the cars had left the property. She pulled out her airwaves set.

"The Jag's on the road, heading towards Southport," she said.

"John, don't let him get away," Jordan said.

Jordan left his own car and headed for Stella's. He glanced from the junction in time to see the white van leaving. He slammed the door as Stella pulled out from the kerb and for just a moment the world became distant again and his vision blurred.

"Seat belt, boss. Seat belt," Stella yelled.

Chapter 74

What were the chances that Beetham was armed? They had no reason to suspect guns were involved. He had been guilty of the most horrible crime. He was a vile human being but that didn't mean he was armed. Jordan glanced across at Stella. She'd lost weight while she'd been away, she was pale and drawn-looking and every so often she coughed from deep in her chest.

He thought he probably had a concussion. The wound on the side of his head wasn't bleeding now but it throbbed and if he raised a hand to touch it, he felt the crusty residue of blood. He knew that once the adrenaline subsided he would be stiff and sore, but for now he was running on chemicals.

Not the best pairing for a difficult arrest.

"I want him, Stel."

"I know, boss. We all do."

"No, I mean I want to be the one to arrest him. I don't want the ART officers to have him. I don't want St Anne Street to do it. I want him. I have to face Mel. I have to tell her how her mother died, and I have to be able to tell her that I caught him, I took him."

"Okay." She glanced across at him and gave a small shrug. "We'll do it. Hang on."

They were heading along College Avenue. "I reckon he's making for Southport and then God knows where. We're coming up to the railway station and I'm going to try and force him to turn into the parking area. Actually, though, we should have permission for pursuit."

"I'm calling this a continuation of earlier, same bloke just a bit later. I was pursuit commander. I might not get away with it but let's just do this."

The van wasn't speeding. Obviously, he didn't want to attract attention.

They were just a couple of metres behind now and Stella flashed her lights. She sounded the horn. He should have no idea that they were on the job, the car was unmarked. She sounded the horn again. She pulled alongside. He might remember them from the yoga class. If so, chances were he would make a run for it. Stella's car could probably take him, but it could get very messy.

Jordan turned away from the window, hiding his face. She flashed her lights again and sounded her horn. Beetham glanced across and gave her the finger. She wagged a hand up and down in a 'slow down' gesture. They were almost at the station car park. Stella fell back.

"Right, this is it. Hang on, boss."

He had no idea what she intended. Not until she put her foot down, not until she sped forward and connected with the rear of the van.

"Don't want the sodding airbags to deploy. Can't give him too much of a crunch. Just want him to turn in."

Her knuckles were white on the wheel, her shoulders tense but she was calm and in control.

"Of course he might just make a run for it."

She sounded the horn again and flashed the lights. She turned on the left-hand indicator then pushed the car forward to thud against his rear bumper. It was working, he was pulling across the road. He was turning into the car park.

As soon as he was off the road Beetham stopped and flung open the car door. He bounced from the van and then leaned back inside and drew out a heavy-looking golf club.

"You bastard. What the hell are you playing at? You could get us killed."

Stella and Jordan were out of the car now and running across the car park.

They saw the moment of recognition. They saw him glance back and forth. He took a step towards them and raised the club. There was a shout from the station platform.

"Hey, what's going on down there? I've called the cops."

Beetham flung the golf iron across the space between him and Jordan. He jumped the narrow crash barrier and sprinted onto the platform. Jordan batted aside the club and staggered forward. Stella was alongside him now.

"I've got him, boss. I've got him," Stella gasped.

It was raining heavily. The station was deserted except for one member of staff in uniform. He stepped forward as Beetham ran across the platform.

"Hey, you silly bugger, what are you doing?" he shouted. "Don't go down there. Don't. There's an electric line. Stop. You idiot."

Chapter 75

Beetham had a moment of indecision. The railwayman dashed forward and stretched out both arms.

"Don't be a fool. It's not safe, don't go down there."

Beetham turned to look at him and then the other way to where Jordan and Stella were almost upon him.

He was wearing trainers with rubber soles. Chances were that even if he stepped on the electric line, he would get away with it. The current wouldn't go to ground, and he would be across the track and away. Jordan leaned and snatched at him. Beetham turned to fend him off.

"Give it up, Beetham. It's over," Jordan shouted.

The other man hesitated, glancing back and forth, searching for a way out.

"Why, man? Why those poor women?" Jordan said.

"Don't be so bloody dim. You know why. Money. What good were they to anyone? That kid, getting her kit off for a couple of pounds a time for old blokes to stare at her. She was worth much more to me, you've no idea. And that stupid old cow. What good was she? No husband, no life to speak of, just hanging around night school and bloody yoga. I was making her famous. She was going to be seen all over the world. She should have been thanking me instead of snivelling and whining."

"You had no right," Jordan said. He had moved closer now and was within an arm's length.

"Right? It's nothing to do with rights. You have to grab what you can, when you can. Everybody does. Don't come any closer." He took another couple of steps backwards. "Look, I'll be gone by tonight. You can keep the CDs, you can have them – make you a small fortune if you find the right market."

"Don't be stupid. You know that's not going to happen. Come on, it's time to go, time to sort it all out and give Jean's family some closure."

"Closure, what do you think I am, some sort of trick cyclist? No, it's over and I'm off."

Stella had sidled around them and he turned to see her moving towards him, closer now than Jordan, almost there. Beetham jerked backwards.

As he started to topple, he reached out his hands groping. He caught hold of Jordan's jacket. Jordan tried to grip his wrist and pull him to safety. Stella jumped the last couple of metres but Beetham was already too far past the point of balance. His skin was wet, and Jordan's grip was weaker than it should have been.

Beetham's fingers slipped and he knew that he was going over the edge. If luck was on his side, he would still

189

be okay. He needed to touch the live rail and make contact with another of the rails to be in trouble.

Luck was not on his side.

He didn't scream. There was no flash, the lights in the station didn't flicker. He was simply dead.

Jordan was at the edge of the platform poised and ready to jump down.

"Wait. Wait, mate, don't do that. There's nothing you can do for him. Let me isolate the section."

As he yelled across, the railway worker was already on his way to the substation. Beetham's hands were locked around the rails, the DC current still running through his body. As the length of track was isolated, they saw him relax.

* * *

The British Transport Police had dealt with this sort of thing far too many times and they had a tried and tested routine in place. Jordan and Stella felt like spare parts. As they sat in the damp of the early morning hours the pain and stiffness made itself known.

"We'll get off as soon as the coroner gets here," Stella said. "I'm taking you to the hospital. You're not right."

Jordan didn't have the energy to argue.

John Grice and Kath had followed the Jaguar back to Liverpool where they had been joined by the ART. The driver had been arrested trying to book travel to Ireland. It had caused quite a furore at the ferry port. David Griffiths phoned Jordan to congratulate him.

"You've done a brilliant job again, mate. Miladdo is already squealing like a stuck pig, trying to make a deal. He's insisting he had nothing to do with the deaths. According to him it was all Beetham and he's fuming that Beetham was selling those DVDs. Not part of the deal apparently and he reckons that's what screwed them up. We're searching the house in Formby and there's evidence of more evil-doing in a basement there. This is going to run for a bit now. It's going international and we don't know how many women have been involved or what happened to them. Plenty to do when you get back here. You're hurt, I believe?"

"I'm okay. Just a clonk on the head. I'll be fine tomorrow. Has anyone been in touch with Mel Barker?"

"Manchester force sent someone to break the news and there's a family liaison officer with her."

"I'll go and see her, soon as," Jordan said.

"You don't have to, mate. It's taken care of."

"Yeah, I do have to."

"As you like. Oh yes, pass on my congratulations to Stella."

Jordan ended the call. He wouldn't do that. He wouldn't pretend that there hadn't been politics at play that had tried to rob her of her first major case at Copy Lane. She'd find out in time. He would try to ensure that she was given the credit she deserved but the virus had muddied the waters so none of it was straightforward, and nobody could claim much credit anyway with Jean and Beetham both dead. Right now he didn't have the energy to think about it.

"Tell you what, Stel, just take me home, will you. I don't need the hospital. I know how to deal with a head injury, I've been hit by a cricket ball a couple of times. If I'm worried, I'll see someone. All being well I'll go and see Mel tomorrow. Do you want to come with?"

"That's not the way I'd put it, but I know I should. I'll pick you up and– Oh!" She suddenly remembered the condition of her car. The front bumper was cracked, and the lights smashed. "Hmm. Probably need a lift, won't we?"

"Oh shit yes, your car. Oh well, I guess you can claim on the insurance – or maybe not, eh?"

"Bloody typical. This is why I can't have nice things." She laughed. "My granny always said you shouldn't be too proud of stuff because it gets taken away. I'll have a word with one of the patrol drivers, cadge us a lift. You sit there and try not to fall over."

Chapter 76

Jordan wanted to stay in bed. Every part of his body was sore, but the grogginess had subsided, and he didn't think he needed medical attention. This morning the bed was warm, and Penny had brought coffee and toast.

"Stay where you are, love. Take a day. You can't change anything now. It all just has to run its course."

He shook his head. "I need to get this out of the way. I owe it to Mel and Jean. I'll take some painkillers. Anyway it's not that bad. I've had worse."

* * *

He didn't go to Manchester. The liaison officer called to say that Mel had decided she needed to be in her mum's house and was on the train mid-morning. Jordan agreed to meet her at Lime Street. Stella went with him, and Penny took Harry to Old Roan to tidy up and make sure there was nothing too distressing in Jean's house. She used the key that had been given to the SOC team.

Mel was calm but devastated, she tried to summon up a smile for them and it was such a brave effort Stella felt compelled to pull her into a hug. It was a mistake. The contact and the kindness undid what little resolve the young woman had left and she sobbed against Stella's shoulder.

"I'm sorry. I thought I'd cried it all out but – ha! – apparently not. I knew this was probably what was going to happen, but it was still a terrible shock. I wondered for a while if she had been depressed and I hadn't known. I did think she might have killed herself somewhere. That made me feel really guilty but, in a strange way, now I wish that had happened. Anything would have been better than this." She wiped her hand across her face and then turned to Jordan. "I want to know everything."

"I don't know whether that's the best idea."

"If you don't tell me everything then I'll imagine things and it will be worse."

Jordan didn't see how anyone could imagine anything worse, but he would do his best to keep with the truth and still be kind.

When they arrived at the house, they left Mel to go inside on her own. Penny was in the garden with Harry.

"I'll get off home," she said to Jordan. "I reckon it would be best if she comes to us, if she will. I'll make dinner and perhaps she'll stay over."

Jordan made a cup of tea that none of them touched as they sat in the living room, Jordan and Stella on the settee and Mel in the easy chair by the fire. She had dragged a soft blanket around her shoulders but still looked hunched and tense.

"Did you know your mum had a heart condition?" Jordan asked.

"Yes. But it was under control. She had medication and it wasn't a problem."

"According to the medical examiner that was the cause of death. She hadn't had her pills. She was dehydrated, and under great stress. She thought of you, at the end." He told her about the name scratched into the wall.

"Had she been raped?"

"No. There was no evidence of that. She had been kept confined, she hadn't been fed, and as I say she was under terrible strain. Listen, Mel, it wasn't nice. She was probably very frightened and in pain, but I don't think there is anything to be gained by you knowing every detail. We are still investigating. In the future you will probably hear a lot of the nastier facts, but you'll be stronger by then and more able to deal with it. Please for now just leave it."

"When can I have her back?"

"It won't be long. I'll make sure they arrange an interim death certificate so that you don't have to wait until after the inquest to have her funeral."

"And him? What about him?"

Jordan felt he was on safer ground now as he related the events. He told her about the flat and what was being done with the films.

"Your mum was part of something much bigger and it was terrible luck that she came into contact with Beetham just at a time when it was hard for him to meet other women. He skated over the discovery of Jean's body and the nasty little lean-to. Then he described what had happened at the railway station.

"Was he afraid?"

"I think he was. He knew he was going to fall. But honestly it was very quick. I won't lie to you. He wouldn't have known much about it really. Just here one moment and gone the next."

"That's a shame. I wanted him to suffer. I wanted him to know fear like my mum had felt, and I wanted him to know he was going to die."

"I understand. I'm sorry, Mel, I wish I could have got you justice," Jordan said.

"Oh, you did. Let's be honest, if you'd brought him in then he might have got a clever lawyer that could have got him off, or just a couple of years put away. Now, I know that he'll never be able to hurt anyone again. I'm glad he's dead and I know that's unchristian of me. I don't care. Actually, I don't think I'm a Christian anymore anyway. The things I've seen in the last few years made me doubt any faith I had, and this has finished it for me. How could anyone treat another human being that way? No. I don't believe in God. But thank you for being honest with me and thank you for getting rid of the filth."

And with that bald statement she began to cry again.

Chapter 77

The following Monday they began to tackle the paperwork. There were reports to prepare relating to the case for the coroner's court regarding Beetham, and the CPS in relation to Rich Moore. Personal reports from those who had been closely involved. Witness statements had to be checked, and chains of evidence and crime scene commentary all had to be verified. They wanted no screw-ups in court. Everyone was focused on making sure that Jean and Mel had justice for the terrible thing that had happened.

"Pub later," John Grice said, and there was a muted cheer.

Okay it wasn't the end they had hoped for, but they had to move on and there were congratulations from the assistant chief constable and DCIs in both Copy Lane and St Anne Street. It would be recorded as a clear-up for them even though there was still work to do with the bigger investigation.

At the end of shift as the team were grabbing coats and bags Stella came to sit at Jordan's desk and told them all they'd be along in a little while. She turned and glared at them, daring anyone to make a comment or even to smirk.

"Not the result we'd have liked," she said when they were on their own.

"No, but a result of sorts, I guess. There's a lot more to be done. St Anne Street are in touch with forces in Europe and up to now we don't know how big this will turn out to be. Rich Moore is a mine of information and he's trying to do a deal to save his own skin. Middle-grade bad guy. He posed as an agent to get poor Maisie out to the community centre. Told her he was a friend of Beetham's from way back. Actually that bit was true, they had a similar background. Anyway, I reckon he's very useful for pointing fingers. When you think about it, grabbing him was more good luck than good management," Jordan said.

"True, but where would we be without luck, if we're being honest? I mean this whole thing with the women overseas – who would have ever thought part of it would be in a bloody community hall in Old Roan? Did you have any idea?"

"How do you mean?"

"I thought the stuff from Serious and Organised was more for information rather than part of a bigger case. But I'm not so sure now. Did you know more than you were letting on?"

"Oh well, I guess the whole thing became pretty convoluted. Anyway, at the end of the day Copy Lane will get the credit for Beetham and Rich Moore and their part in it."

"Copy Lane, not me?" she said.

"You know what I mean. All of us. The team, I guess."

"Hmm. Maybe. Anyway, I suppose you're off back down to the city now. Are you going to be involved with the ongoing inquiries?"

"That's the plan and I want to see that through, but I don't know about afterwards. The way I feel right now, I'm not sure I want it."

"How do you mean?"

"I'm not sure it's really what I want to do. These big cases, I know they are higher profile but being a small cog in a big wheel doesn't suit me that well. Looking for Jean, speaking to Mel, even though it ended so tragically, it was more real somehow. Anyway, I'm taking some leave. I really need to go down and see Nana Gloria. They keep telling me she's okay, but I need to see for myself. Then I might take Penny and Harry away for a bit. We haven't done anything for such a long time. This case has made me realise again just how important family is. Well you know that. You're close with your lot, aren't you?"

"Yes, I am, even though they get on my tits sometimes. You sound quite low, mate."

"I guess I am a bit. I failed. I know some good came out of it and we stopped a bad guy, but it's still going on and Jean Barker is dead forever. Oh, I don't know. Perhaps I'm just tired."

"Maybe. Come on, turn off your computer and give Penny a ring, tell her you'll be late. We'll get a taxi. Let's go and get bladdered, Jordan."

"Yeah."

"Thanks. You're a good mate." She leaned and gave him a peck on the cheek.

The End

List of characters

Detective Sergeant Stella May – Liverpool born and bred. Lives in Aintree.

Detective Inspector Jordan Carr – Jamaican heritage. Married to Penny. They have one baby – Harry.

Nana Gloria – Jordan's granny.

Detective Chief Inspector David Griffiths – Serious and Organised Crime.

Keith Young – Stella's neighbour. Tenant of the upstairs flat. Physiotherapist at the Royal Hospital.

Jean Barker – Missing woman.

Melanie Barker – Jean's daughter and friend of Penny Carr from university.

Detective Constable John Grice – Newly promoted detective.

Steve – Geek from the digital forensics department.

Detective Chief Inspector Josh Martin – In charge at Copy Lane.

Veronica Surr – Yoga teacher.

Billy Tranter – Bargee.

Maisie Brewer – Model.

Brian Beetham – Caretaker at the community centre.

Kath and Vi – Junior officers.

Karen – Josh Martin's secretary.

If you enjoyed this book, please let others know by leaving a quick review on Amazon. Also, if you spot anything untoward in the paperback, get in touch. We strive for the best quality and appreciate reader feedback.

editor@thebookfolks.com

www.thebookfolks.com

Also by Diane Dickson:

BODY ON THE SHORE (Book 1)
BODY BY THE DOCKS (Book 2)
BODY OUT OF PLACE (Book 3)
BODY IN THE SQUAT (Book 4)
BODY ON THE ESTATE (Book 6)

BURNING GREED
BRUTAL PURSUIT
BRAZEN ESCAPE
BRUTAL PURSUIT
BLURRED LINES

TWIST OF TRUTH
TANGLED TRUTH
BONE BABY
LEAVING GEORGE
WHO FOLLOWS
THE GRAVE
PICTURES OF YOU
LAYERS OF LIES
DEPTHS OF DECEPTION
YOU'RE DEAD
SINGLE TO EDINBURGH
HOPELESS

Other titles of interest

OUT FOR REVENGE by Tony Bassett

There's a noticeable change of atmosphere in the city of Birmingham when a dangerous prisoner is released. He has plans to up his drugs business. But someone will quickly put an end to that. Detective Sunita Roy has the unenviable task of hunting down the gangsters who were likely responsible. But when the cops close in, they'll have an even bigger problem than they first imagined.

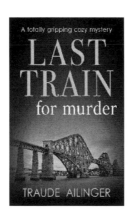

LAST TRAIN FOR MURDER by Traude Ailinger

An investigative journalist who made a career out of sticking it to the man dies on a train to Edinburgh, having been poisoned. DI Russell McCord struggles in the investigation after getting banned from contacting helpful but self-serving reporter Amy Thornton. But the latter is ready to go in, all guns blazing. After the smoke has cleared, what will remain standing?

Printed in Great Britain
by Amazon